MW01602018

This is Not Love

Vahe Berberian

This is Not Love

WET PAINT

Published in the United States of America

Book design by Stephan Nave
Cover painting by Vahe Berberian
Edited by Jaime Brockway

www.vaheberberian.com
vahe.berberian@gmail.com

Printed in the United States of America
by Wet Paint Publishing.

To Leon

1

"At a certain age, looking backwards, everyone considers their life as if it were a novel where he is the hero," said Max Frisch. I don't know who the fuck Max Frisch is, and I sure as hell haven't begun to write this book – if one can call it that – because I have the audacity to believe that my life can make a good novel. I am not a writer. As a matter of fact, I have no formal education, and English is my third language. My first language is Armenian. My parents hardly ever agreed on anything; however, they both believed that speaking our mother tongue was essential in becoming not just worthy Armenians, but also decent human beings. My second language is French, because I was born and raised in Paris. English is my third language, and I learned it mostly after moving to Los Angeles at the age of twenty-two. That makes Turkish my fourth language, since my mother, who was born in Istanbul, spoke mainly Turkish with my grandfather, who had survived the Armenian Genocide of 1915, had lost every single member of his family and spent his childhood in the streets of Istanbul without getting a chance to learn the language of his people.

Even though my intention is to tell the truth and nothing but the truth, I know very well that all truth is subjective. Every thought is tainted by one's experiences and beliefs, and the idea of remembering events in detail, especially conversations, is incongruous and absurd, to say the least. However, I have promised myself to be as honest as humanly possible. Fortunately, the story I am about to tell you is etched in my brain, the scar of the branding still sore and the smell of the singe still lingering in my nostrils.

I am not exactly sure when I first realized that living with myself was like carrying a package bomb at all times – a lethal weapon that could kill on a whim, almost always unintentionally turning me into a murderer. I am a dangerous man, a very dangerous man, because I am a silent, invisible killer. Even if one day I decide to confess my crimes, no one would believe me. As a matter of fact, they would probably ridicule me and dismiss me as a pathetic lunatic. That is exactly why I have gradually built an impenetrable shell around me, narrowed my circle of close friends, kept people – especially women – at a safe distance, buried myself in my work and made a name for myself as a conceited, eccentric artist who is lucky enough to live comfortably through his art, surrounded by an aura of mystery.

That aura was not there yet when Lisa and I fell in love. We were young, reckless, and eager to get married, and in hindsight, we both knew that the marriage wouldn't last, but we went ahead anyway. Four years later we parted ways amicably, promising to stay friends till death do us part. And yet, it was *life* that did us part, and we slowly forgot each other's existence.

At twenty-eight, I allowed my divorce to put the final nail in the coffin of my dreams of having a family. One by one I shut all the doors and windows of my emotional edifice. Occasionally people tiptoed in unnoticed but never stayed long enough to be able to get on my nerves or upset me enough to experience the consequences of my censure. So, I have no idea how, at the age of fifty-two, I allowed a complete stranger to walk into my life, nestle in my heart, make a home for herself, take over my entire existence, and awaken the criminal inside me that I thought I had locked away for good.

I met her at the opening of my exhibition at the Art Attack Gallery on La Brea. I had been waiting for this exhibition for nearly five years, and by the time the gallery was ready, my enthusiasm had faded, and doubts about my work had crept in. So, it was a pleasant surprise to see the gallery bustling on the opening night. Old friends, acquaintances, long-lost faces, fellow artists, aspiring talents, distant relatives, collectors, art enthusiasts desperate for something to admire, and staunch art critics hunting for something to criticize… they were all there. And, to my greatest astonishment, I was happy to see them all, genuinely happy – or as close to happy as someone like me can be.

I socialized, signed catalogues, posed for the cameras, and downed shots with my gallerist Roland, who had brought a bottle of single malt Glenlivet just for me. By the time my friend Harry was ready to drive me home, I was intoxicated enough to make lunch plans with half a dozen people and promise to reach out to a string of women I had crossed paths with over the past two decades.

In an attempt to freshen up, I stumbled into the bathroom with an intoxicated grin plastered on my face, swaying from side to side. I relieved my bladder and then, standing before the grand, ornately framed mirror, I splashed ice-cold water on my face. Running my damp fingers through my thinning, gray-streaked hair, I made sure a strand strategically hung over the right side of my face. Yes, time had taken its toll on my hair, but fuck it, I still believed I possessed a striking appearance for my age:

tall and relatively fit, despite my disdain for exercise. Sure, the effects of booze and cigarettes had etched themselves onto my face, giving it a weathered, leathery texture that exuded a rugged allure. I was a modern-day Clark Gable, with loops adorning my ears, silver bracelets clinging to my wrists, and hefty rings arming my fingers. The tattoos that crept below my wrists completed the image. And, of course, I was drunk.

Breathing in a satisfied sigh, I nodded approvingly at my reflection and sauntered out of the bathroom, fully intent on finding Harry. However, I was intercepted by two young women along the way. The tall, slender blond, exuding classic Eastern European beauty, seemed uneasy in her high-heeled shoes. She nudged her friend and playfully pushed her toward me. The friend, a petite brunette with captivating blue eyes, timidly smiled and extended her hand, saying something. The narrow corridor leading to the main gallery hall was packed, the noise drowning out her words. "Say that again?" I shouted, keeping her sweaty fingers in my grasp.

"I'm Kylie," she replied, raising her voice to be heard.

I was too wasted to recall my response, but I distinctly remember sensing a strange familiarity in her crystal-blue eyes. I believe I asked if we had met before, but I can't be certain. What I do remember is her asking if she could visit my studio sometime. While I can't recall my exact words, I must have given her the impression that it was a possibility, perhaps hoping that she would bring her girlfriend along. At some point I must have shared my phone number, because two weeks later, I received a text from an unknown number: "Are we still on?"

"Who is this?"

"Kylie."

"Kylie who?"

"Kylie, the girl you met on your opening night. I was there with my friend Luna."

"Yes, yes… I remember," I assured her, even though I had no idea who she was.

"So, I'll see you in an hour?" she asked with a delayed question mark.

"Sounds good," I said, having decided to ride the exhibition's wave and say more yeses than noes.

An hour later a text popped up: "I'm here."

Typical, I thought. Only a millennial would text when they're right outside, instead of giving a simple knock on the damn door.

As I swung the door open, a vague image of her face formed in my mind, and a tingling sensation stirred within me.

She stood there, slightly shorter and much younger than I remembered, clad in tattered jeans, black Converse sneakers, a white top, with a backpack hanging off her right shoulder.

"Come on in."

"Thank you so much for the invite. I'm so glad we're doing this."

"The pleasure is all mine," I said pulling her in.

Kylie tiptoed through my studio, twirling around with a bemused, fascinated expression. "Wow, this place is incredible. I always wondered what it'd be like, but it's even better than I imagined."

I swept my gaze across the studio, feeling a sense of contentment. This old warehouse, once a printing company's domain, had become my sanctuary. It was where I lived, slept, and worked. Some people venture out into the world, but I bring the world to me. I hardly left my studio, but I kept its doors open to friends from around the globe, who came to pop in or spend a few weeks. That's why Lee used to call it Julian's Mecca. Everyone on Abbot Kinney knew who I was, and even those who didn't recognize me still wore polite smiles, convinced I was someone worth knowing.

The studio had been passed down to me by my friend Lee, my landlord and one of my earliest collectors. Lee was the slightly older, Black, Rasta version of myself. Tall, handsome, always adorned in white linen suits and an abundance of silver necklaces, bracelets, and jewelry he designed himself. In fact, half of the jewelry I wore I inherited from him after he succumbed to AIDS at the age of forty-eight. During his last three years, I played the role of his guardian angel, shuttling him to doctors, hospitals, and exams and enduring the hellish shopping expeditions. And when he withered away, I literally carried him from my car to his wheelchair and from his wheelchair to his godforsaken bed.

"Wow, look at all these books. There must be hundreds of them," Kylie remarked, her eyes scanning the wall-to-wall library at the far end.

I nodded modestly.

"Have you read all of them?"

"Almost."

"How about this one?" Kylie pointed at a slim book titled *How to Say No.* "Have you read this one?"

"Well, my friend Lucy gave that to me years ago, saying, 'You absolutely must read this.' And naturally, I couldn't say no."

Kylie let out a chuckle. "I love reading, but I don't think I read enough." She took a few more steps, twirled, and then paused. "I hope you don't mind, but I brought a couple of paintings with me… to get some feedback. You can look at them whenever you want."

"Where are they?" I inquired.

"They're right here, outside the door."

"Bring them in," I said with an uncharacteristically joyful gesture, then helped her carry them inside. There were seven pieces, all painted on medium-sized cheaply stretched canvases. "Let me see. Put them up against the wall."

"Now?" she asked, a hint of nervousness in her voice.

"Why not? Don't be nervous. I couldn't be harsh even if I tried," I assured her, settling into my worn-out, paint-stained armchair facing the wall.

Kylie carefully placed the paintings on the floor, leaning them against the wall, and stood beside them, arms akimbo, like a guilty child waiting to be reprimanded.

"Do you smoke?" I asked picking up a roach from the ashtray.

She playfully shook her head, a familiar smile playing on her lips. It was a dangerous, foretelling smile.

"How about a drink?"

Kylie shook her head and laughed. "Too early. I have somewhere to be in an hour."

I took a long drag from the joint and, crossing my legs, asked, "So, when did you do these?"

"They are all recent pieces. A few months old."

They were vibrant, busy, haphazardly done works, with an undeniable charm that betrayed the talent of an emerging artist. I nodded in silent approval, then asked, "How old are you? Twenty-three?"

Kylie pursed her lips and let out a laugh. "Close, I'm twenty-four."

"The perfect age. Old enough to feel independent and young enough to feel reckless."

"This one is an earlier piece," she said, gesturing to the last painting in the row. "As you can see, my work used to be more figurative."

"Interesting."

Kylie shrugged, disappointed.

"By 'interesting,' I don't mean it in the way Americans often do, as a euphemism for 'meh... nothing special.' I do find it intriguing," I clarified.

"That's my friend Jeff." Kylie motioned toward the painting.

Jeff, a faceless figure, sat on a stool, holding two balls in his hands. Despite the bold and brash brushstrokes, there was an underlying serenity in the piece.

"This is good. I like it a lot," I said realizing that my reactions were too subdued to be encouraging.

Her eyes lit up. "Really? I thought this would be your least favorite piece since it's so figurative and so different from your own work."

"Well, it's very good," I replied, now fully aware that I was stretching the truth just to see that delightful smile on her face.

"That makes me very happy," she said, grinning from ear to ear. "So that's Jeff. The ball in his right hand represents..."

"Don't explain," I interrupted. "You really don't need to explain. Your job is to paint, and the viewer's job is to appreciate it. Let the viewer see whatever the hell they want. You can talk about your creative process or your language as much as you like, but don't explain the piece itself."

She nodded like an obedient student and hugged herself tighter.

"Who's Jeff, your boyfriend?" I asked, surprised by the tinge of envy in my voice.

"We were together for two years, but we're not seeing each other anymore."

"Why not?" I immediately regretted asking the question, feeling embarrassed, but she didn't seem fazed by it.

She simply shrugged. "I don't know. We just decided to take a break."

Realizing that I hadn't said much about the other works, and feeling a need to say something, I expressed my appreciation for them, though I added they were a little too crowded for my taste. "Of course, that has a lot to do with your age," I acknowledged. "When you're young, you're bound to use a lot of colors. Young artists are like kittens."

"How so?" she asked, intrigued.

"Kittens eat whatever you give them until they develop their own preferences," I explained. "Once they know what they like, that's all they eat. Artists are very similar. When you're young, you experiment with all kinds of colors. You're full of energy, arrogance, and a desire to show off. But when you mature, you know exactly what you like. You develop a certain taste and you stick with it. For instance, there are certain colors I never use anymore."

Kylie listened, a hint of cynicism playing on her face, probably taken aback by the animated way I spoke. If she thought I was a little nuts, it suited me just fine. I enjoyed playing the role of the eccentric artist.

"Like what kind of colors?"

"Purple, magenta, light green, or turquoise, for example," I replied. "Thirty years ago, I would buy around twenty colors in tubes when I visited an art store. Now, I find myself grabbing only six or seven colors in gallons. That's all I need."

"But I love your old works," Kylie pouted her lips.

"You and a whole bunch of others who think my work has become too minimalist and monochromatic."

"But I also love your new pieces," she added, laughing.

"Thanks. But honestly, there are certain pieces out there that I would gladly buy them back and burn them. I didn't like them then and I don't like them now. I only sold them because I needed the money."

"Why would you burn them?" Kylie asked, with a crooked grin on her face. "Why do you want to be so dramatic?"

"Well, I love drama," I laughed. "Also, there's something purifying about burning a piece. On the other hand, there are some works out there that are so good, I think I would never be able to repeat them."

"Well, the ones we have at home are beautiful. I'll never let you touch them."

"You have some of my works?" I asked, taken aback.

Kylie was astonished by my surprise. "Of course. We have a whole bunch of your early works. We have six large pieces, and the rest are mostly sketches. My mom kept them after you guys divorced."

It took a while for the words to sink in, then it hit me: the eyes, the mouth, the smirk, the familiar mannerism... it was Lisa. Now I understood why she had looked so eerily familiar the moment I had laid eyes on her.

"You're Lisa's daughter?" I stammered.

"What do you mean? You know I'm Lisa's daughter," she said, genuinely confused.

"Lisa... my ex-wife, Lisa?"

"Yes. That's the first thing I told you when we met."

"You never told me," I said, now almost amused by the predicament I was in.

"I did. I did!" She laughed, swaying her head back and forth. "But you probably were too drunk."

"What did I say?"

"Nothing."

"You told me you're Lisa's daughter and I said nothing?"

"Yes, and I was surprised," said Kylie, continuing to laugh.

"Well, your mother always accused me of being too detached from reality," I said, taking a drag from the roach. "I still can't believe it. The last time I saw you, you were nine? Ten? You don't remember, do you?"

Kylie shook her head and reached for my roach.

"Un-fucking-believable! I should have known," I said, genuinely tickled. "And you live with your parents?"

"Yes. I just moved back in. I don't mind, though.... They're okay. I can do what I want..." she said, coughing up the smoke.

I held her chin in my fingers, rotated her face, examined it up close, then sat back. "How is your mom?"

"She's okay. She's good. When was the last time you saw her?"

"Years ago. I can't remember. How are your grandparents?"

Kylie pouted her lips and shook her head.

"Both of them?" I asked, feeling a pang of genuine pain. She nodded.

"So, Maya is gone?"

Kylie gave another nod.

"She was one of my favorite people. I loved your grandmother. It makes sense. Your mother's Scottish blue eyes and your grandmother's Dutch Indonesian olive complexion..."

Kylie offered a warm smile, her arms wrapping tightly around herself.

"For some reason this piece is growing on me. I really like this one. It's a good piece," I said, indicating a smaller piece just to break the awkward silence.

Kylie thanked me with a slight bow.

"So, what exactly can I do for you?" I asked, immediately resenting the tone of my voice.

"I want to intern for you," said Kylie, staring at me quizzically.

"Trust me, my dear, there's nothing good you can learn from me."

Kylie smirked dismissively.

"Do you value happiness?" I challenged.

"Excuse me?"

"Do you want to be happy?"

"Sure. I think everybody wants to be happy, no?"

"If your goal in life is to find happiness, then you're on the wrong track. Go do something else. Art and happiness don't mix well; they're like oil and water. Art is a messy business, and I'm not saying this based on the old romantic notion of the suffering artist. Art gnaws at you from inside, it eats you up, it drains you. An artist is like a candle – if you want to illuminate, you must melt. If you work in a bank or, let's say, in a real estate office, you know that the harder you work, the better you'll be rewarded. You know exactly what to do and how to get ahead. But if you're an artist, there are no guarantees. You'll work day and night, bust your ass, put everything you got into it, having no idea if your work will be appreciated," I said, assembling bits and pieces from a talk I had given a few weeks earlier at the gallery.

"I'm telling you, if you want to be an athlete, you have to have the body, the physical constitution for it. And you want to be an artist, you have to have the emotional constitution for it. If you don't think you can endure rejection, poverty, or criticism, or if you can't handle baring your soul to your audience, then throw away your paints and brushes, go to Italy for two weeks, visit the museums, get drunk with friends, have fun, and then go back to school and get your graduate degree in something else. Because at thirty-five or forty, when you realize that you haven't made it, it will be too late. You would be too old to start a new career."

Kylie's smile froze on her face. She blinked a few times, then shrugged.

"I'm sure you have a job, right?" I inquired.

"Yes. I tutor two kids three days a week. But it's only part time."

"So whatever money you make, you'll spend it on canvases, paints and brushes, and then one day you'll start resenting the fact that your friends are wearing better shoes and clothes. Eventually you'll say, 'Fuck this, I want to enjoy life too…'"

"I don't care about clothes and shoes," Kylie interrupted. "I want to be able to paint. That's what I love, and that's what I want to do."

I nodded, probably because I felt I had been too harsh with her. During the ensuing long silence, Kylie inspected an old unfinished painting against the wall near the door. "I love the texture of this one," she said, touching it with her index finger, then turning to me. "Look, I don't need to get paid. I can come two or three times a week, and I promise you won't regret it."

I pretended to think, but somehow, I already knew I would assent.

She stepped closer, stood before me, her head tilted coyly. "Please."

I felt both her arm muscles with my fingers. "You know I work on large canvases. It's serious physical labor. Underneath each painting are at least ten or twelve layers. Years of the same repetitive movement with these heavy brushes have really fucked up my right shoulder. After working for an hour, I have to ice my back, take ibuprofen for the inflammation, and rest. Can you do that kind of work?"

Kylie gave a series of quick, uninterrupted nods. "Sure, I can. I lift weights. I'll wrestle you any time."

"I really don't think this is a good idea," I said, stepping back. Maybe it was a strategic move on my side, an unconscious effort to extend her flirtatious pleas.

"Why? Why isn't it a good idea?" Kylie pressed.

"Do you want me to be very honest with you?"

"Yes, of course."

"It's not a good idea because... I know myself too well. Sooner or later I will try to sleep with you. I will attempt to seduce you, and if I succeed it's not going to end well. And if I fail it's going to be even worse. Either way, one of us, or may be both of us, will get hurt. Trust me."

Kylie kept shaking her head with a dismissive sneer.

"You could be my daughter, for Christ's sake," I almost yelled.

"But I'm not," she retorted even louder.

"I can't be a good mentor anyway. I'll be a bad influence. I'll corrupt you and then your mother.... I can't even imagine what your mother will say."

"Nothing. She'll say nothing," said Kylie, now visibly upset. "I thought you liked having people around when you work."

"Who said that?"

"You did. I watched a documentary about you on YouTube. You said your studio is a hangout for young, gifted people. You said, 'I love company, as long as I don't have to entertain them. I process everything that happens around me and incorporate them in my work.'" Kylie stopped;

her tongue slipped out of her mouth, wetted her lips, and disappeared.

"That must have been a very old interview." I smirked.

"Mom said you always had people around."

"What else has she told you about me?"

"Not much. Good things in general. You should come and visit them one day."

I smiled and nodded, knowing full well that I would never do such a thing.

"So why can't I just come and hang out?" Her doggedness was irksome yet disarming. "I can come three times a week."

"What about your job?"

"I don't care about my job. It's only a few hours a week anyway." She examined my stare. "I won't talk much."

"Don't worry, I'm the one who talks too much," I assured her.

"That's okay. I'm a good listener. I'm not a kid, okay. I'm not this fragile, delicate woman who will bow submissively and allow you to do whatever you wish with her. If you're worried about the fact that you won't be able to handle me, I can understand that. But if you're worried about me... I would say you're too full of yourself."

I had probably forgotten her mother's brash impudence. "I can't believe how uncanny the resemblance with your mother is. The way you laugh, the way your lips curve, the way you stand... You're the new, improved version of your mother, with her same audacity."

"My dad says the same thing," she said mustering a smile. Then she began to resolutely collect her things. "Okay, I'm not going to force you. You have my number." She stacked her paintings against the wall, near the door, then, standing erect, closed her eyes. "Wow. I think I'm stoned."

"Sit," I said, offering my chair. Then I picked up a brush and began to paint, probably to fill the awkward silence or keep the brush from dying out.

"Can I help?" She slouched in my chair.

"Have some water and relax."

"I can paint that coat," she rose, reaching for the brush.

"Not with what you're wearing. Where there is a drop of paint, there is always a blotch. You should know that," I cautioned.

"I do, trust me. I have ruined so many fucking dresses I love. But I don't mind if I get these clothes dirty," she said, reaching again for the brush.

"Next time."

"Really?" Hope sparkled in her eyes.

I shook my head, smiled, and dropped my brush in the bucket of water.

2

I am a murderer, a killer who doesn't need weapons. It may sound far-fetched, but trust me, all it takes is a mere desire to cause someone's death. It all began when I was still a child. My first victim was Madame Olivia, our plump, bespectacled, red-haired geography teacher. I must have been around nine or ten years old. She accused me of cheating during an exam. Despite my attempts to convince her otherwise, she not only disbelieved me but also ridiculed me in front of the entire class and sent me to the principal. I felt so humiliated that I prayed for her death before going to sleep that night. I wished for it with all my heart, and surprisingly, three days later, she died in a car crash on her way to Normandy.

My mother's boss at the Galeries Lafayette became my second victim. Not long after we lost my father to a sudden heart attack, my mother took a job in the women's shoe section of that famed department store. The job weighed on her spirit. Her boss, Monsieur Edmond, was the sort of curmudgeon who took pleasure in others' misery, regularly sending my mother home in tears. One Wednesday, my elder brother, Vahan, his face grotesquely distorted from a vicious toothache, picked me up from school. We were to go to the store to meet our mother, who was to escort him to the dentist. When we got there, my mother, her face stained with tears, told us that Monsieur Edmond denied her an early leave, fully aware of her prior appointment. I remember seething with anger as I walked home, trailing my brother along Boulevard Haussmann. I prayed fervently for Monsieur Edmond's demise, believing that my clenched fists would seal the deal. Sure enough, a few days later, my mother came home teary-eyed, bearing the news of Monsieur Edmond's stroke-induced death at the department store. When I asked her why she was upset, she explained that Monsieur Edmond might have been insufferable, but rejoicing in another person's death was not in her nature.

By the time I was fourteen, there was Emile, the neighbor who spat at me, called me an idiot, and accused me of stealing his bicycle. Emile met his end falling from his family's fourth-floor balcony. Then there was Nona, my second girlfriend who had cheated on me; she succumbed to cancer at nineteen. And Michel, the gallery owner on Bastille who had refused to pay me for my three large paintings he had sold, drowned during a summer vacation in Nice.

Years ago, I calculated fourteen victims during a drunken stupor, which led me to swear never to count again, especially given the mounting coincidences and seemingly random deaths. Had I inadvertently caused Lee's death, one of the kindest people I knew, solely to inherit his studio? I hope not. Brought up by a devout Christian mother, I initially attributed these incidents to divine intervention, but when I lost faith in God at fifteen, I opted to believe in mysterious coincidences. By my twenties, I had reached the unsettling conclusion that – as bizarre as it might seem – I possessed a lethal power that would linger for the rest of my life. What's even more unnerving is that as I grew older, killing became all too easy. All it took was a wish.

Was my being a murderous bastard the only secret I kept from Kylie? I am not sure, but I know for certain that everything else was trivial compared to my perpetual fear throughout our relationship that one day, unwittingly, in a moment of rage, I would wish her death.

It's mind-boggling how certain situations can telegraph their outcomes from the very beginning. That night, hours after Kylie's visit to my studio, sleep eluded me. I knew, or rather was certain, that letting Kylie into my life was a grievous mistake. Yet I was also aware of the fatalistic undercurrent to the situation and how futile it would be to resist it.

In the initial couple of months, Kylie paid me two visits per week. These visits gradually became more frequent, and soon she was a permanent fixture in my studio. It felt as though she had been a part of my life all along. My studio was the ideal habitat for her; she belonged there from the moment she stepped in. She was warm, funny, witty, and a fast learner. She took over priming my canvases, washing brushes, painting over large areas that needed concealment, and even organizing the digital photos of my paintings. We shared meals, drinks and, most important, laughter.

I taught her to prepare Armenian coffee, relishing her scientific precision in measuring water, in ensuring the coffee boiled three times, and in carefully filling the demitasses. I delighted in the way she sipped her coffee, determined to enjoy it despite her grimace. Her secret smile was ever present, as if she knew something but chose to keep it to herself. I adored how she would walk into the studio, toss her backpack onto the rattan chair near the door, and greet me with a hug and a kiss on each cheek. Then, she would don her plaid flannel painting shirt, tattered jeans, and sneakers. I found her ritual of removing her silver ring and fixing her hair into a bun with a thin brush endearing.

She often forgot her ring on the sink, only to pick it up the next day and forget it again. I loved the way her body moved when she painted, like a dance, and her intermittent pauses to close her eyes and appreciate the music that always filled my studio. I loved the way she sprawled on my armchair contemplating. I loved her high-pitched laughter, initially jarring but eventually charming, and most of all the analytical attention she paid to me when I spoke, always ready with questions and counterarguments.

Above all, it was the sense of familiarity and intimacy that drew me in from the moment I first saw her in the gallery. It was probably her fourth visit when we agreed to be brutally honest with each other – a pact sealed with a handshake. This was supposedly before we fell in love. But even then, as we shook hands, we both knew that it was an impossible promise to keep.

How honest were we with each other? Mostly, I'd say, as we both understood that sometimes honesty can be self-serving and not worth the pain or heartache it can inflict on the ones we love.

The day we shook hands, holding onto each other's palms for a few moments longer than mere friends do, I should have disclosed to her that I was a dangerous man, someone who couldn't be trusted. But… I didn't. I failed to confess then, and I also refrained months later, when, intoxicated by love, we pledged an eternity to each other while hanging on every word spoken.

Honestly, I'm not certain whether I ever tried to resist falling in love with Kylie. I suspect that from the moment she stepped into my studio, I had already decided to let fate lead the way. It was as though I had opted to drive a car, fully cognizant that it lacked brakes. Things might have veered in a different direction had I unveiled my deepest secret to her. She might have considered me utterly insane and vanished from my life forever. The reality is there's no definitive way to predict the outcome.

On a Tuesday afternoon, Kylie walked in, looking radiant in a short, white, flowy dress and combat boots. Her hair was styled in a haphazard updo, contributing to a deliberately disheveled look.

Harry, who had dropped by to persuade me to visit his studio and scrutinize his new works, was occupying my table, sketching with oil pastels while I toiled over a large canvas affixed to my wall. A committed bachelor, Harry, a few years my senior, resided in a compact two-bedroom apartment in Eagle Rock. He barely made ends meet, selling his paintings mainly to empathetic friends aware of his circumstances and willing to lend support. He had an older brother in Canada who occasionally offered financial aid, but their relationship was distant. After losing his mother to old age, Harry had transformed the spare bedroom into a studio and was earnestly seeking a gallery to represent him. Every gallery he had approached had rejected him under some pretense or another. However, he always maintained his sense of humor and showed no signs of bitterness toward life.

"I don't think I'm going to work today," announced Kylie as I admired her from head to toe.

"Why's that?" I asked.

"I'm leaving in an hour. I told you yesterday, I'm going out with my friend Suzan. She's visiting from New York."

I nodded and resumed my work. Kylie prepared some coffee, shared a few laughs with us over Harry's crass jokes, assured him that she would take me to his studio soon and, after his departure, sat silently with me, observing the painting I was engrossed in.

"I think you're going somewhere very interesting with this one," she commented, standing up and collecting the coffee cups. "And I'm not using 'interesting' in the typical American sense," she added, with a wink.

"I'm thinking of painting over it."

"You're going to? Why?" she asked, perplexed.

"I don't like it. Something's missing," I replied, stepping back from the piece.

"I wouldn't touch it. Especially not this part right here," she advised, pointing at the upper right corner of the canvas.

"I like that part too," I confessed. "And that's precisely why I'm going to paint over it. Remember lesson twelve: if there's a particular part in a painting that you adore, but the rest doesn't resonate, the first thing you should do is erase the part you love. Paint over it. Otherwise, you'll spend an eternity trying to save that fragment while working around it. So, it must go. Trust me, it will immediately give you a feeling of liberation. And don't worry, you'll always have the ability to re-create that part or come up with something even better."

"Here, let me do it," she said, picking up a brush and the small bucket of white paint.

"You'll ruin your dress."

"No, I won't," she assured, setting to work. "How many layers are there underneath this?"

"I have lost count, but as you can see, none of the layers are really completely lost."

"It's like drawing on a chalkboard," she remarked. "No matter how much you erase, the traces of the previous drawing will always be there."

"Exactly! And that's what gives the piece a sense of history. Essentially, you're creating history. See the richness of the texture? It's gaining volume. Nothing is lost," I said, inhaling from the joint in my hand.

Kylie stopped. "I don't like it when you smoke. You lose your edge."

"I have cut down," I lied.

She sneered. "You also promised to exercise every day."

"I've spent my entire life hoping that scientists would one day announce that we've had it wrong all along and that exercise is, in fact, harmful," I countered.

Kylie scoffed, shook her head, and went back to work.

"You know what Picasso said. 'I despise innocent pleasures.' What's a person without a vice? I've been sublimating far too much as it is."

"What do you mean?"

"Sublimation is the process of diverting your impulses into socially acceptable behaviors. Art thrives on sublimation. For instance, right now, I'm most likely sublimating my desire to sleep with you. I'm transforming my lust for you into a painting," I declared, immediately regretting my choice of words.

If my intention had been to shock her or solicit an emotional reaction, I had failed, because Kylie responded, entirely unfazed, "So... like... every painting is an orgasm you never experienced..."

I nodded. "More accurately... every painting is an orgasm transformed into a painting."

"I'm assuming that's the ideal situation..." Kylie retorted skeptically, watching me pour a glass of scotch. "Then why the constant need to smoke and drink?"

"Consider the job of a banker," I suggested, taking a gulp of the whiskey. "Every morning you have to report to work with your faculties fully engaged. You need to be logical and alert to make sound judgments. In our line of work, it's the exact opposite. An artist needs to be in an altered state to sideline reason and rely on his unconscious.

This accelerates that process. To liberate yourself from inhibitions and truly give your all, you must continually push your boundaries."

Kylie pursed her lips and shrugged. "Or maybe it's just an excuse to kill your liver. I think there are other ways of letting go or putting your unconscious to work."

"You're right – probably this is the easiest way to shed my inhibitions or cross the boundary between life and art to make me feel that what I'm doing really matters.... Because deep down inside I know very well that it really doesn't. Do you have any idea how much bodily fluid ends up on canvases? Sweat, blood, piss, semen… I used to masturbate on the canvas all the time when I was younger."

"Why not now?" Kylie's smirk had vanished.

"Why not? Well, I still do, but painting is no longer a separate experience. After all these years, I've managed to mold my life into a form of art. Painting, eating, smoking, making love, it has all blended into a singular experience. There was a time when painting meant everything to me. Now, if I realize that spending three hours with Harry might have a positive impact on his life, I'll say fuck the painting; Harry needs me more than the canvas does. You can't take art too seriously. You can't sanctify it. Some of the greatest artists and art aficionados were major assholes," I claimed, taking another swig of my drink. "There is so much vanity in art anyway…"

"Vanity? What makes you say that?"

"There is something inherently vain in being an artist. You paint, then you give an exhibition inviting people to come and check out your work. You're saying, 'Here, look at what I do!' You write a book, get it published, and you expect people to read it. Art is inherently exhibitionist because it thrives on spectators. You can have the most mesmerizing voice and sing like a fucking nightingale, but without an audience, you're not really a singer. That's just how it is."

Kylie shrugged. "I don't agree. I don't paint for others. I paint for myself."

"That's a mantra of a failed artist. No one creates purely for themselves. At some point, everyone seeks some form of validation."

Kylie paused, studying me for a long moment. Opting to withhold her thoughts, she dropped the brush into the bucket of paint, then slouched in my chair. Her right leg draped over the chair's arm, she tucked her skirt between her thighs and assessed her work. "The layer might be a bit too thick, don't you think?"

"It's good. I love the different shades of white and the drips you've created," I assured, massaging her shoulders. "I think I know where to take it from here."

"I just wish I had diluted the paint a bit more to create a more translucent coat." Kylie mulled for a moment then gave a nod of satisfaction.

"Lesson number eleven: always, and I mean always, rinse the brush in water. Never leave it in the paint, and never leave the lid open."

"But I do. I always do. And for your information, after twelve comes thirteen, not eleven." Kylie's tongue peeked out for a split second before disappearing. She then sprang up. "Okay, I think I better get going."

I wrapped her in a hug from behind, my hand resting on her crossed arms. Together, we observed the still-wet white canvas. Perhaps we were both pretending to do so, because I certainly felt her heartbeat racing as fiercely as mine. I took a deep breath, relishing the scent of her freshly washed, lavender-scented hair. I gave her a gentle squeeze and was about to step back when she unexpectedly spun around. Our lips brushed against each other in a fleeting kiss. It was a transient, almost imperceptible contact, and I reflexively retreated, yet the damage was done. Had it been a mere mishap or a calculated move toward a kiss? Her enigmatic eyes offered no answers. She looked up, flashed a mysterious smile, and gracefully walked away, leaving me in a state of utter disarray.

3

I began writing this story by emphasizing that I am a painter, not a writer. So why am I writing? Voltaire believed that writing is the painting of the voice. I am painting with my voice because I can't paint this story with a brush. And if you're wondering why I need to tell it, my answer would be… for the same reason birds sing, women menstruate, and jalapeños cause hemorrhoids. I wake up because I can't sleep forever. I have my breakfast because I can't live without eating, I drink because my body needs water, I piss because if I don't, my bladder will burst, I sleep because it's impossible to stay awake more than a few days, and I tell this story because it's simply impossible to go on without making sense of it at all.

It's a Tuesday or possibly a Wednesday morning. The sun has yet to make its appearance. Nowadays, my routine includes waking up around 3 a.m., feigning sleep for another couple of hours, and then forcing myself to get up and take a stroll.

As I pass the old hippie pseudo-commune down the street, I spot a young man in a Robin Hood costume getting into his car.

"Hey," he waves. "Good morning."

I realize it's Derek, the screenwriter who's constantly seen walking his dog. "I'm doing the Renaissance Fair," he explains with a weary chuckle, justifying his appearance.

"Good for you," I respond, instantly feeling alienated by my own words. 'Good for you.' One of the earliest phrases I picked up from Lee. 'Good for you.' I suppose I'm suggesting that his participation in the Renaissance Fair doesn't elicit any emotional response from me. I feel neither joy nor sorrow, but I conjecture that it must be beneficial for him.

A simulated smile clings to my face as I draw in the crisp morning air and observe a seagull squawk overhead.

Dead man walking… with an absurd smile on his face.

Kylie was conspicuously absent for the next two days. My entire time was consumed by thoughts of her, devoid of any inclination to work or engage in conversation. I resisted the impulse to reach out to her via a call or text. When she eventually showed up at my doorstep, backpack slung over her shoulder and an armful of books in tow, she acted as though nothing had transpired. Her cheerfulness was infectious, and her geniality made me discard any resolutions I had made about confronting her and clarifying that whatever had happened – if indeed anything had – was a mistake and should not be repeated.

Throughout our customary coffee ritual, Kylie disregarded the incessant buzzing of her phone, and when she finally glanced at it, she shook her head and rolled her eyes in frustration.

"What's the matter?" I asked.

"It's fucking Jeff. He's driving me crazy," she vented.

"What does he want?"

"I don't know," she said, visibly frustrated. "I saw him on Monday for, like, a couple of hours, and now he won't stop calling me."

An unexpected pang of jealousy hit me. "So, what does he want?"

"He's in love and says he wants to be with me. He seriously wants to marry me." Kylie rolled her eyes.

"And you're not interested?"

"No!" she exclaimed, her eyes wide in mock horror. "I'm not ready for a commitment like that."

"Why not? You love him too, don't you? You'll get married, have a couple of kids, and forget this... this insanity."

"Sure, become an ideal housewife, share photos of my kids on Facebook and Instagram, and write mommy blogs."

"Why not?"

"Because that's not what I want. That's a cop-out. If you do that, no one will expect anything more from you. You'll get all the 'likes' and trick yourself into believing that by raising decent kids, you're making a substantial contribution to society." Kylie briefly stuck out her tongue and shook her head with a sense of urgency. "Speaking of which, I truly think you should consider setting up a Facebook and Instagram profile." "Thanks, but I don't think I need them. I already have a Facebook page, but I never use it."

"You definitely need an Instagram account. It's important to keep people informed about your work. That's the only way to stay connected with your followers. Stop nodding, Julian. You need to keep pace with the times."

"Fine. I'll think about it," I conceded, rising from my seat. "I'm starving."

Kylie took a sip of the dregs of her coffee and pulled a face. "I've been meaning to ask, why did you marry so young? You were just twenty-two, right?"

"Twenty-three. Younger than you are now, and your mother had only just turned twenty-one."

"Why so young?"

"Because we didn't know better. We were in love, and we thought love would conquer all. Obviously, we were mistaken. Your mother was wild and beautiful, which turned out to be a dangerous combination."

"I wish I could've seen that wild side of her," Kylie said, with a dismissive shrug. "So, what happened then?"

"Well, we went our separate ways, and she ended up with custody of the children we never had."

Kylie waited for me to continue.

"I really don't feel like talking about this now."

"Did you fall in love with anyone after my mother?"

"After the great love there are minor ones, like an earthquake followed by aftershocks."

"Do you miss my mother?"

"Okay, enough. I'm going to go get us something to eat before we get any visitors," I said, grabbing my keys.

"God! You're hardly ever alone. I don't know how you manage. My mom is your polar opposite. Sometimes she goes days without seeing anyone."

"Well, your mom is very comfortable in her own skin. She's always been like that. Me, I should never be left alone with my thoughts. I drive myself crazy. For me, there is no silence. There is always me whispering in my ear, making myself miserable," I said, making my way to the door.

Kylie caught up with me. "Whispering what?"

"All kinds of things, like the mole on your back is cancerous, your chest pain is a sign of an imminent heart attack, there is no sense in doing anything, everything is useless.... So, I substitute that voice with a more pleasant one, like yours, and it makes life a little more bearable," I said, placing a soft kiss on her forehead. "So, what are you in the mood to eat?"

"I'm not hungry."

"Lesson number 12, don't wait until you're hungry to eat. When you're famished, you tend to overeat. That's why

I eat three times a day, like clockwork, morning, noon, and night."

"But I can't eat when I'm not hungry."

"Trust me, try it for a few days and you'll get the hang of it."

"Okay, I'll eat on one condition. We'll go eat out."

I stopped, pretended to consider the proposal, then nodded in agreement.

Jack, of Hagop's Kitchen, was thrilled when we walked in. "Man, it feels like ages since I last saw you," he said, giving me a warm embrace. Then he planted a kiss on Kylie's cheeks and thanked her for dragging me to him.

"How do you know I dragged him?" Kylie asked, trailing Jack to our table.

"Because I know he never goes out. There was a time when this was literally his kitchen. He was here three, four times a week. Now he hardly shows up," Jack explained, directing us to a table near the kitchen counter. He shot Kylie a prolonged, flirtatious look. "And he's always with the most stunning women."

Kylie feigned a disapproving glance at me and nodded knowingly.

"With friends like you, who needs enemies," I quipped, giving Jack a friendly thump on the back.

"So, what are we eating?" Kylie inquired, scanning the surroundings for a menu.

"Whatever he feeds us."

Jack winked at her and vanished into the kitchen.

A young waiter brought us two beers and retreated.

"Aren't you glad you got out of the house?" Kylie asked, a twinkle in her eyes.

I smiled.

"What? Admit it. It's good to be out."

"But I do get out."

Kylie playfully stuck out her tongue. "When was the last time you stepped out that wasn't work-related?"

Jack played some music and flashed a thumbs-up from behind the counter. I reciprocated with a smile and a wave of gratitude, even though I would have much preferred silence.

"Why do you insist on having music while you paint?" Kylie asked.

"Does it bother you?"

"No, I'm just curious."

"I can't paint without music. For me, painting is like dancing. When I was very young, I painted with my fingers. As I matured, I began using my wrist, then my elbow, later my shoulder, until finally I was painting with my entire body. It took me years to master this dance of colors, and now painting is a rhythmic ritual for me. And one does not dance without music."

"You can, if you really want to."

"Perhaps, but it's more vibrant with music. I believe you can transform anything into an art form if you infuse it with a dance."

Kylie took a generous sip of her beer, then began to sample some of the meze on her plate.

"What are you reading now?" I asked, breaking the long silence.

"Maurice Nadeau's *History of Surrealism*."

"You are?"

"You recommended it."

"Good. It's a fantastic read. When you're done with it, I want you to read *Archeology of Madness*."

"What's it about?"

"It's about Komitas, the most significant Armenian composer, who went mad during the Genocide in 1915 and spent the rest of his life in a mental institution in Paris."

Kylie grimaced slightly. "You keep on giving me heavy, depressing books."

"It's okay. You can do it. You can handle it. I just want to know how the fuck do you manage to read so fast? I don't get it."

"I know," Kylie responded with a touch of pride. "And I don't miss a single line."

"Bravo! I'm genuinely proud of you. I wish I could take some credit for the person you've become, but that wouldn't be fair. Your mother has done a phenomenal job. It's her achievement."

Kylie put down her fork, gently placed her hand on mine, and held my gaze. "But you have. You've done so much."

I squeezed her hand and smiled gratefully.

"I love you," she declared, as casually as if she'd said "This beer is cold" or "Tomorrow is Thursday."

Returning to the studio, I carried on with the painting that had been tormenting me for the past few days, while Kylie worked on the computer, cataloging photographs of my artwork.

I felt disoriented. An emotional numbness overwhelmed me, and I was uncertain how to react. Me, the old wolf, who had traversed the vast expanses of love with brash assurance, was now floundering. The prospect of altering the course of our relationship, and thus potentially losing her, was terrifying. Kylie, however, didn't seem the least bit troubled. She was her usual vibrant, chirpy self, playfully teasing me, imitating my accent, and subtly pushing the boundaries of our closeness.

41

Kylie stood up, turned down the volume on the sound system, and eased back into her chair. "You know, you've mentioned before about not explaining your work. I've been giving it some thought. If someone lacks a genuine understanding or appreciation of art, wouldn't it be more advantageous for them to hear the explanation from the artist rather than rely on their judgment?"

"Explain what?" I queried, not pausing my work. "What can you explain when there's nothing to be explained? In my younger days, my pieces had figures in them. Every time people recognized the figures, they would exclaim, 'Oh, I see… it's a man and woman.' Or, 'Oh, I get it, it's a woman cradling a child.' And I'd ask, understand what? If my aim was to depict a man and woman, I would have done just that. I guess it's impossible for people to observe a painting without seeking a reference point. You should approach a painting just like you listen to music. Do you ever listen to music and think, 'What does it resemble?' or 'What does it remind me of?' No! Do you ever question a composer about the meaning behind their music? No! You take it for what it is."

"It's funny you say that," Kylie responded, grinning. "Just a couple of days ago I saw a program where they were showing how these starlings – birds – when they sing, they sound exactly like Mozart. They were saying that Mozart had a pet starling, and he was very attached to it and was heartbroken when his bird died."

"Really? I had no idea. Well, Mozart might have been influenced by his starling, but never once have I listened to Mozart and thought, 'Wow, I love this music because it reminds me so much of a bird chirping.'"

Kylie took a deep breath. "So, you are saying that when you paint you have nothing in mind."

"Precisely," I retorted, a wave of enthusiasm washing over me as I sauntered toward the kitchen and poured myself a glass of whiskey. "If I had a predetermined notion, that wouldn't be painting; it would be illustration. When I paint, I try to keep an open mind, absorbing everything that happens to me, everything in my surroundings. I don't paint ideas; I paint abstract emotions. What propels me is the turmoil within… and it's not feasible to pinpoint what exactly that turmoil is at any given moment. It's an amalgamation of everything that transpires inside me – politics, relationships, rage, affection and, of course, my muse."

Kylie snatched my glass, took a sizable sip, grimaced, and handed it back. "Who's your muse?"

I took a beat to ponder the source of her question. I was uncertain if the question sprouted from personal intrigue or a creative perspective. "At this moment, I couldn't say."

"Maybe that's why you don't feel as creative as you want to be. Maybe you need a muse."

"Maybe," I murmured absentmindedly.

"But what exactly is a muse?"

"For me, a muse is someone you love so much that you create in order to impress or charm them. It's like saying, 'Look, my love, look what I've painted for you. Now can I fuck you?'"

Kylie's reaction was a knowing nod, indicating that she had likely heard me express this sentiment in a previous interview.

"How many muses have you had?" she asked.

I scratched my four-day stubble and pretended to ponder. "I have no idea. Quite a few."

"Was my mom one of your muses?"

"Of course. I was madly in love with her. I married her and never wanted to marry anyone else after her."

"Why?"

"Because once is enough," I said, struggling to conceal my impatience. "I never envisioned sharing my life with someone else."

Kylie nodded wistfully, her fingers persisting on the keyboard. I watched the dance of her digits, leaned over to kiss her, and then retreated to my armchair, fixing a blank stare at the canvas. A few minutes later Kylie paused typing. "Did you ever want to have a baby with my mom?"

"We were young and we thought we had eternity ahead of us," I said, scrubbing my fingers with a rag."

Kylie resumed typing, then stopped again. "So, when does a muse stop being a muse?"

"Enough with the questions."

"Just one more for today," she insisted.

"Fine, what do you want to know?"

"When does a muse stop being a muse?"

"I suppose a muse stops being a muse when they cease to be impressed by your work. When they become jaded or decide they've had enough of the existential angst from an artist and no longer wish to suffer."

"Or when you get tired of them and find someone else to impress?" Kylie posed, her gaze probing.

I did not answer. I shrugged noncommittally, took a sideways glance at her, and walked away.

"So how come you don't have a muse right now?" Kylie called out after a prolonged silence.

"That was your last question, Kylig. Keep the rest for another day."

"Come on, please, we're having a conversation," pleaded Kylie, mimicking my French accent.

"That's precisely the point. We're not getting anything done."

"Well, this is important to me. Remember, you're my mentor."

"I never agreed to be your mentor. In fact, I specifically told you that I will never be your mentor. You're here to learn from me just as much as I am from you."

"I have nothing to teach you."

"Of course, you do, Kylig."

"Kylig... Is that the diminutive for 'Kylie'?"

"Yes. In Armenian, we create a diminutive of a name by adding an 'ig' at the end."

"Ok, Julig," Kylie retorted instantly. "Or is it 'Julianig'?"

I erupted into laughter. "And you know what 'Kylig' means in Armenian?"

"What?"

"A little wolf, a cub."

"Really? I love it."

I tried to refocus on my painting, but her uninhibited nature, wild, disheveled looks, tan, and dirt-streaked bare feet were too distracting.

"So, you genuinely think you'll learn something from me?"

"Absolutely. Trust me, I've already learned a lot," I replied, avoiding her gaze. "Each time you pose a question, it forces me to self-reflect and express my thoughts, and leads to new realizations." I exhaled a deep breath, my eyes drifting toward Lee's outdated 1960s clock near the door. Pulling Kylie into a close embrace, I rested my chin on her head. "I think it's time to wrap up for the day. I'd like to rest a bit before the gang arrives. It's belote night, remember."

"What's belote?"

"It's a card game we play in France and the rest of the Mediterranean countries."

"You're going to play cards again?"

"What do you mean 'again'? You know Tuesdays are our belote nights."

"Well, then, I'm going," she declared, her lips pouting like a petulant child.

I planted kisses on her head, neck, nape, and shoulders, stopping when I noticed goosebumps on her neck. "Okay, this is torture. I need to stop." I gave her one last kiss on the cheek and headed toward the long, orange sofa under the window. I flung myself on it and closed my eyes, my head propped up on the armrest and my right leg hanging over the edge. A few minutes later, I felt Kylie's ripe lips on mine, followed by her whispered goodbye.

I yearned for another kiss, but instead I heard Kylie's receding footsteps, followed by the heavy metal door's resounding slam.

The belote game had ended. Ara, Jacques, and Haig were still lounging around the table, enjoying their cigars, when my cellphone rang. I didn't plan on answering, but seeing Kylie's picture made me instinctively press 'Answer.' Unknown to me, Kylie had set her picture in my contacts: a silly cross-eyed photo with her tongue sticking out.

"What are you up to?"

"Nothing. The guys are still here," I replied while rummaging for a lighter among the glasses, playing cards, beer bottles, and ashtrays overflowing with cigarette butts.

"Okay, then I'll let you go," Kylie said, hanging up promptly.

A rush of restlessness overtook me. I lost interest in the table's conversation, leaned back, and relit my cigar. I couldn't wait for my friends to leave so I could call Kylie and hear what she had to say. About half an hour later, Haig finally stood up. "I don't know about you guys, but I'm done for tonight."

The rest of the gang followed suit.

"By the way, congratulations, Haig. I hear Helen is pregnant," said Jacques, picking up his jacket.

Feigning surprise, we showered Haig with congratulations, even though he didn't seem overly thrilled. "I don't know, man," he admitted, his head shaking in weary resignation. "It wasn't my idea. I thought we had a deal, but at forty-two she changed her mind, and she wants a child."

"What? You're not ecstatic?" Ara inquired.

"I suppose I am, but I genuinely question whether it's wise to bring a child into this world."

"For the sake of posterity, at least," Jacques, a father to two adolescent boys, offered.

"Haig shook his head. "Posterity? Honestly, the whole posterity thing doesn't mean much to me."

"I can't believe you're saying that," said Ara, sliding the deck of cards back into its box.

"Listen," said Haig. "You know the name of your father, right?"

Ara gave him a nod.

"And, of course, you know the name of his father?"

Ara gave him another nod.

"And the name of his father? Do you know it?"

Jacques thought about it for a second. "I do, but I can't remember it at this very second."

"See?" said Haig, smiling. "That's how far back your posterity goes. Who cares what you leave behind? All you do is collect more stuff for your kids or grandchildren to clean up after you're gone."

"On that note, I think I'm gone," said Jacques, and the gang followed.

I immediately picked up the phone and called Kylie. "Hey."

"Did they leave?"

"Yes. They're gone," I said, as I began to undress. "What are you doing?"

"Nothing. I was reading."

"I'm glad you called."

"Really?"

"Yes, really."

"Listen," said Kylie with a twinkle in her voice. "This afternoon, when we were talking, you never answered my question. Why is it that you don't have a muse? You're always surrounded by all these women, and yet there's no one who inspires you?"

"What do you want me to say? For me, every woman is a different city. One might be a seaside town, warm and welcoming, another might be green, cold, and foreboding yet beautiful, and yet another can be a Middle Eastern city, crowded, loud, and nostalgic.... I find beauty in almost every woman. I visit them, I live in them for a while, but I have not found one where I can move and settle."

"What about me?"

"What about you?"

"What kind of city am I?"

"You're a baby," I chuckled nervously. "You're like a scene in a postcard someone has sent – a beautiful virgin island I will admire from afar but will never visit."

Silence.

"You think I'm a virgin?"

"Of course not. I meant that figuratively. I want to keep the postcard on the refrigerator and imagine living there, but I know I never will."

"Why do you say that?"

"Because you're fucking twenty-four years old. At my age, if I were to live on your island, I might get stranded there. I'd either starve to death or be devoured by some predatory creature. I'm too old to survive on your island." I lit a cigarette and took a drag. "Are you there?"

"I'm here," sang Kylie. "Listen, why didn't you have kids with my mom?"

"Haven't we discussed this?"

"I think you would have made a good father."

"Maybe. I think at one point I thought of having kids, but then I lost interest. Now I understand why ascetics, shamans, and gurus don't have children. Because when you have a child, all your love is directed toward that one person only. But when you have no children, you start adopting everybody you meet. One way or another, in all my relationships, men or women, eventually I find myself playing the father."

Silence.

"Have you been hurt?"

"What?" I was feeling tipsy, and a slight headache was creeping into my forehead. "What's the question?"

"I was asking if you have ever been hurt."

"Of course I have, but why are you asking?" I got up and walked to the kitchen.

"I don't know. I'm just curious. Did my mom hurt you?"

"Of course she did, and I hurt her back. I told you, we were young and wild and angry. We thought we could love and be free at the same time. We were fighting anything and everything that smelled of capitulation or compromise. We thought we were rebels. We were crazy about each other, but we could never trust one another, so we did all the wrong things to spite each other." I downed a large glass of water and shuffled back to the sofa.

"Like what? What kind of things?"

Exhausted, I slumped onto my sofa, struggling to keep my eyes open. "Kylig, in retrospect, do I regret it? Sure, I do. And I can't stand people who say they have no regrets, even though one of my favorite songs is Edith Piaf's *Non, je ne regrette rien.*"

"But that doesn't answer my question."

"Jesus, Kylig, I'm tired. What do you want me to say? We both fucked up. Do I regret it? Yes, of course I do. If there was a way of regretting on your mother's behalf, I would do that, too, but I guess I can't, so that's that." I closed my eyes. The room swirled around me and my nausea intensified. "Listen, I have to go. I'll see you tomorrow."

"Okay, I love you."

"I love you too," I responded, the phone still glued to my ear long after it had fallen silent. Had I just reciprocated an "I love you" sincerely? When was the last time I felt something akin to this? Me, who had an aversion to squandering time on phone calls but just spent over 45 minutes conversing like a fucking teenager. Why did it give off the feeling of flirtation? This wasn't healthy. I wasn't prepared for this – especially not at my age and certainly not with a twenty-four-year-old who could be the closest equivalent to the daughter I never fathered. I needed to nip this in the bud before one of us became irreparably wounded. What perturbed me most was the unease and fear that engulfed me each time I contemplated her. I, the practiced flirt, the womanizer, the master of commitment-free relationships, the Houdini of love, was now fearful of a young girl who had stormed into my life, wreaking havoc. All these years, I had managed to control my emotional life, just as I had my environment. I took pride in knowing that within my chaotic studio, I knew exactly where every paint pot, brush, rag, canvas, frame, book, and piece of clothing lay; there was a method to my madness. I similarly took pride in having managed to compartmentalize my emotions over my fifty-two years, keeping them sorted and unblemished, free of complications. In the ocean of love, I had been a skilled swimmer, had dodged many treacherous waves, swam great distances, and always returned unscathed, if somewhat smug. Could that be the problem? Had I become too self-assured for my own good? My father used to say that most drowning victims are good swimmers – they drown due to their overconfidence.

The lingering smells of cigar smoke and whiskey vapors clung to my nostrils as I dragged myself to the bathroom, collapsing to my knees before the toilet to throw up. With my arms braced on the toilet bowl and my head hanging low, nearly grazing the water, I continued to vomit, the world spinning around me. It's strange, I thought, how at times like these one yearns for a touch of tenderness and love yet feels fortunate to be alone, spared the humiliation of a witness to their pitiful state.

4

These morning walks are doing me good. I have a feeling if I keep it up I might die a healthier man.

Stepping out of the house a half hour later than usual, I find the streets more vibrant than ever. A striking woman, carrying a small plastic bag filled with dog shit, walks past me. I search for the dog, but it's nowhere to be found. I love L.A. Two houses down from Derek's dilapidated abode, I spot three burly, disheveled construction workers in yellow vests, perched on a barrier sipping coffee from their thermoses. As I stroll by, I catch a snippet of their conversation. "Your moon is in Cancer, in the fourth house, bro. That means you're a nurturing, sensitive man. Don't let her treat you like that." I love L.A. Blanketed by a heap of garments, a homeless man snoozes at the entrance of the Marvel Shop. A grimy, dark hand clutching a phone protrudes from beneath the pile. I love L.A.

In two hours, my friend Lucy will swing by for breakfast. She's resolute in her mission to pull me out of my rut. I'm sure she's going to nag me for not seeing a therapist. She insists that I should be on antidepressants for a while. I suppose I'll lie and tell her I've already begun taking them. Rabih Almandine, *habibi*, I sincerely doubt you believe that if existentialists had antidepressants at their disposal, we'd be spared a great deal of tedious literature. Consider the glut of dull literature created by those cheerfully numbed by medication. Were existentialists on antidepressants, the libraries of 1950s Paris might be brimming with self-help books. Dostoevsky could have been running a lively casino, and Sartre might have opened a popular restaurant on Saint-Germain. Let's face it: Why would one write if not spurred by despair, or at least a persistent melancholy?

In the ensuing weeks, Kylie's presence grew to encompass my entire life. She brought her canvases or used some of mine to paint at the studio, made plans for both of us, took me out, drove me to the beach, to exhibitions and parties…. In no time, she became an extension of myself. Even my initially skeptical female friends were charmed by her. She cooked for them, entertained them, and soon they affectionately addressed her as Kylig. She was a regular fixture on my street. Occasionally, when it was too late to drive home, she'd stay the night in my studio, always on the sofa, donned in one of my T-shirts, curled up in the fetal position, her perpetually warm feet peeking out from under the short woolen blanket.

We existed, or at least I did, in a constant state of equilibrium – always treading a precarious line. I'd often find myself looking away, struggling to resist temptation, yet her comfort with her own body made it impossible not to be captivated. She'd change clothes in my presence, pee with the bathroom door ajar, and strut around draped loosely in a towel after a shower.

Her presence became an addiction. Then, one day, she performed one of her disappearing acts on me again, this time vanishing for an entire week.

I couldn't remember a time in my life when an absence had become such a torturous presence. Two days after her departure, I woke up to find a pair of Kylie's paint-splattered, black-and-white Converse sneakers haphazardly discarded near the sofa by the partition separating the kitchen. The sight was a punch to the gut, causing my eyes to brim with tears. I felt a sense of ridiculous shock and had to concede to myself that I had fallen in love. Her absence had transformed me into a pathetic being – lonely, humiliated, and stripped of dignity. I found myself frantically calling and texting her dozens of times a day. Initially, my messages were casual inquiries and expressions of missing her. Two days later, they morphed into impatient pleas and expressions of worry. By the fourth day, they had turned outright angry, punctuated by exclamations of disbelief and bitter accusations.

I was in the middle of an interview for *Artoon's* online magazine when Kylie silently made her entrance, greeting me with a playful wave of wiggling fingers before tiptoeing into the kitchen. My interviewer was Linda Hernandez, a pleasant middle-aged woman with a heavy-set frame. She had fastened her tiny camera on a tripod and was firing off a barrage of questions at me.

"You mentioned that art is essentially a series of mistakes," Linda interjected, her long eyelashes fluttering as she blinked rapidly.

"Yes, for me, art is a series of mistakes. I once told this to a jazz pianist friend of mine, and he said, 'Funny you say that. We often say jazz is a series of miraculous recoveries.' Well, this mindset significantly influences my creative process, ridding me of any fear. The realization that my work is fluid and can be modified at will infuses it with a certain rawness, an edge."

Linda smiled, blinking thoughtfully. "It would be fascinating to live one's entire life like that."

"Yes, it would. I think art is more about deconstruction than construction, about subtraction rather than addition. Antoine de Saint-Exupéry said perfection is attained not when there is nothing more to add, but when there is nothing more to take away. He probably learned it from the Japanese, but it's true. You must know how to erase. Whenever I'm dissatisfied with a painting, I simply erase it. I paint over it, knowing that nothing is ever truly lost."

Kylie returned with a cup of coffee, leaned against the narrow wall partitioning the kitchen, and began to watch. For a moment, I lost my train of thought, and an awkward silence ensued. Sensing that I had nothing more to add, Linda changed the direction of the conversation. "So, have you applied this philosophy to your life as well – living without fear or hesitation, confident in your ability to alter or amend your actions whenever you wish?"

I took a long self-conscious pause. "I wish. I wish my life was a massive canvas where I could simply paint over any action I regret. But it's never that simple. Most of the time, I find myself terrified of life's irreversible nature. As I grow older, I'm more conscious of the fact that I can't afford to make more mistakes, because I really don't have much time to rewrite my own history. All I can do is try. I try... I'm sorry, I'm rambling."

"Oh no, you're doing fine," Linda responded, rising to her feet. "Would you like some water?"

I shook my head. "My thoughts are too fragmented."

"Don't worry. Most of this is going to be used as voice-over anyway. It's going to be edited over the footage shot in the gallery."

I nodded absentmindedly.

"You were elaborating on your creative process," Linda said, attempting to draw me back into the dialogue.

"The creative process… It's painful. Painful and messy. It's like thrusting your finger in your throat and throwing up. I've always believed that producing great art has little to do with aesthetics or beauty. It's the honesty of a piece that makes all the difference. Life is like a banquet where you walk around tasting a sandwich here and an hors d'oeuvres there, and you drink and drink until your body can't handle it anymore. So, you thrust your finger in your throat, and you throw up. Whatever you have consumed is spewed out: your political affiliations, your loves, the books you've read, the music that inspires you. It's all out in that vomit. You can't hide anything."

Linda gave a satisfied nod, perhaps recognizing that I was paraphrasing one of my old artist statements.

I went on. "After every major creation there is a period of adjustment, which is characterized by insecurity. Fuck, I sound like a textbook!"

Kylie furrowed her brows, signaling me to continue.

I shook my head, indicating my reluctance to elaborate further.

"So, where do you believe that insecurity stems from?" Linda inquired.

"Well, the insecurity comes in when you start asking yourself if there's anything else left in you or if you will ever be able to create again. Because basically you feel empty inside, completely drained. You have spewed your guts out, and there's nothing left to throw up. This is when you know you must start consuming again. You have to rock the boat, fall in and out of love, suffer through anxiety attacks, and eventually get pregnant again in order to give birth, to create."

"Why create at all?"

"Well… the older I get, the more I understand that there may not be a concrete reason for creating. Fellini once said asking him why he makes films is akin to asking a hen why she lays eggs."

Kylie mischievously grinned and stuck her tongue out.

I attempted a smile, then got up. Realizing the interview was over, Linda also stood up and turned off her camera. "This was really insightful. Thank you so much."

"I'm sorry if I seemed a bit off today," I responded, embracing her warmly. "Thank you for your patience."

"Are you kidding?" Linda began to pack up her camera gear.

As I headed toward the kitchen, Kylie wrapped her arms around me from behind, resting her head on my shoulder. "I miss you so much."

I gave her a rigid nod, then gently tapped her hands, signaling her to let go. "Linda, meet Kylie. Kylie, this is Linda, one of my favorite art critics."

"I don't really consider myself an art critic," Linda said, shaking hands with Kylie. "I write for an e-mag, *Artoon*. You may have heard of it."

"Oh yes, of course," Kylie responded, embracing Linda with a kiss on each cheek. "Can I get you some tea, coffee, or something cold?"

"Oh, no, thank you. I should get going. I have to pick up my three-year-old from my sister's place."

After seeing Linda out, I walked back in the studio to find Kylie going through some of my canvases stacked against the wall.

"Nothing new?"

I shook my head.

"This is interesting," she said pointing at an unfinished piece.

"I'm still working on it," I said, sitting at my table.

Kylie gingerly pulled out my chair and sat on my lap

with her arm around my neck. "Are you upset with me?"

"Why should I be upset with you?"

"You are upset," said Kylie, planting a kiss on my cheek.

"Why should I be upset? Just because you haven't called or shown up for a whole week?"

"What's the big deal?"

"What's the big deal?" I asked, doing my best to keep my cool. "Do you have any idea how many times I've tried to reach you? I was worried sick about you."

"You had no reason. I told you I was going to San Diego."

"For a day! You said you were going for one day!"

"Well, my friends wanted me to stay, so I stayed with them." Kylie continued to peck my cheek with kisses.

"What friends?"

"Friends." She shrugged. Then, realizing I wasn't satisfied with her answer, she added, "I was with Luna and Jeff."

I gave a long, silent nod. Somehow, I had expected to hear the name 'Jeff' in the sentence.

"What?"

"Nothing."

"Don't say nothing. Obviously, there is something."

"I thought you said you weren't seeing Jeff," I muttered, against my will.

"I'm not. I mean, I wasn't, but Luna's uncle has a huge house there, and she wanted me to go, and I couldn't say no."

A completely unfamiliar sense of jealousy swept through me. A jealousy so foreign that it took a while for me to recognize it.

"All you needed to do was give me a call and say you're not coming."

"I didn't know you would be worried," said Kylie, exasperated. She stood up and began rummaging through the canvases again. "You haven't been working at all. God, you haven't even washed the brushes."

"I didn't feel like working," I admitted, my voice carrying a note of petulance, like that of a child starved for attention.

Kylie immediately picked up on my self-pity. "Oh," she cooed, assuming a nurturing tone. "Look at you, still upset." Holding my face gently in her hands, she landed a lingering kiss on my lips. "Aren't you excited? Your show was outstanding, the response was fantastic, you sold so many pieces, and there's a massive exhibition coming up. What more could you want? Come on, get up. You need to paint."

"Why? Who gives a fuck? Art hasn't changed anything and never will."

"Really? Are you serious? Your art has impacted so many people I know. You inspire them. They love you. All my friends are envious because I get to spend so much time with you."

"Do you have any idea how much bullshit is entangled in art? By the time you sift through all that, there's barely anything left. You seem to think that there's something sacred and noble about art. Well, let me tell you, there isn't. You want to be a famous artist? You're going to have to play the game, smile and nod when some incredibly wealthy buyer purchases your art, feeding you some fabricated story about how he earned his fortune cleaning toilets or how if you really bust your ass, you can make it too. He'll lay his hand on your shoulder, telling you patronizingly that he's buying your work because he loves supporting artists. What do you do? You smile awkwardly, and your agent averts their eyes, hoping you don't say something to jeopardize the sale. And if your rent is overdue that month, you might even find yourself agreeing when they claim war stimulates economy, or there's no such thing as racism or sexism in this country. Bullshit flows from studios to galleries and from galleries to homes and museums. Art critics and historians wade in the shit, fishing for dollars, all in the name of art. What we create is merchandise, darling. Art is the process of creation, not the residue of the experience." Kylie was staring at me, taken aback, a sardonic smile on her face. "I bet you're thinking, after all this, why does he still paint? You know why I paint? Because it's all I know. If you want to be a successful painter, learn the ropes from someone who's also a businessperson. I never was. Your mother always believed I lacked ambition, but you, I know you'll make it. You're ambitious, you have clear goals, and you know how to chase them. As for me, all I know is how to paint."

"Can you please shut up? I want you to shut up," Kylie said, holding my face in her hands.

I dropped my gaze. "Last night I figured out what your painting is all about."

"Which one?"

I gently moved her off my lap and, picking up the most figurative painting she had brought during her first visit, I leaned it against the wall. "This one."

"Yeah? What's it about?" Kylie asked with a hint of a smirk.

"Well, as you suggested, this represents Jeff, your boyfriend. He has no face because you didn't want to define him as a specific person. He is a nonentity. He's sitting there, posing for you, because you put him in that spot and you want him to remain there, waiting, hoping you'll return to him one day, or occasionally, just to assure yourself that he's still there. The two orbs he is holding in each hand... I'm still pondering their significance. They're peculiar. Their sole purpose seems to be to keep him still. If he had a face, his expression would be one of confusion. 'What the fuck are these, and what am I supposed to do with them?'"

"Wow! You're really upset with me, aren't you," said Kylie, finally dropping the playful act.

"No, I'm more curious than upset. I'm just trying to figure you out."

"Why do you want to figure me out?"

"Because I want to see what's coming," I said, desperately trying to conceal my anger. "I want to understand and predict your behavior. Because I don't like surprises. I really have a hard time dealing with unpredictable people."

"I think we need to be a little unpredictable, otherwise we would be very boring."

"I'd rather be boring…"

Kylie cut me off with a kiss on my lips.

"You think…"

Kylie continued to peck me with kisses.

"As human beings…"

Another kiss to shut me up.

"Will you let me talk?"

One long kiss to take my breath away.

"Listen," I said, pushing her gently and returning to my chair, "in every relationship…"

Kylie followed me, sat on my lap and covered my mouth with her fingers. "Don't talk. Shush. Get up and paint. This is exactly when you should be painting."

I tried to open my mouth, but Kylie immediately pressed her lips to my lips to shut me up. A minute later we were kissing, passionately, almost wrestling – sucking, pulling each other's hair, groping, heaving, and panting.

"I love you," she kept murmuring every time she pulled her face away to gasp for breath. "I. Love. You."

My cock, stiffened in my pants, was desperately trying to find room to expand. As she tried to take off my shirt, Kylie grappled me, bit me, and scratched me. My brain kept on ordering my body to resist, but my penis had raised the flag of rebellion, and the rest of my body followed it by kissing, heaving, fumbling, undressing her, and in a matter of minutes I was inside her. Still sitting on my lap, wrapped around my waist, she quivered and slithered, flailing in spasms, pressing my face against her wet chest. There was something clumsy and oafish about the whole thing, making it obvious that she also had lost control of her body and was trying very hard to leave the impression that this was not foreign territory for her. Clasping her dripping body in my arms, her taut, perky nipples in my mouth, I kept gasping for air. My fingers sculpted her slippery frame as my entire body went through a current that electrocuted us both as we howled, yelped, and died in each other's arms.

We stayed motionless for an eternity, trying to savor every second. When I realized that the door of the studio was not locked, I slithered out of her and made an attempt to stand, but she clutched me in her arms, dripping on my thighs, and bit my shoulder hard enough to draw blood. I made another attempt to rise, but my legs were too weak to support us.

"I need to lock the door," I said, trying to disengage from her.

"No," she countered mischievously.

"Someone might walk in."

Kylie finally stood up, our lips still locked, then helped me to my feet. Together, we walked to the door, secured it, and then made our way to the bed.

Kylie woke up after I'd been painting for a good two hours.

"I can't believe you're not playing music," she said, lounging on the armchair in front of the painting.

"I didn't want to disturb your sleep."

She was barefoot, clothed only in one of my worn, paint-splattered T-shirts. "I think you're done," she declared. "I definitely believe you're done."

I took a few steps back and eased onto her lap. "Something's still missing."

"I think it's perfect. Don't touch it."

"You think?"

"What difference does it make? Regardless of what I say, you're going to paint over it anyway."

"You're probably right."

Kylie bit my arm fiercely. "If you're not content and feel the urge to paint, then put this one aside and start on a new canvas. Otherwise you'll ruin this one, just because you're in the mood to paint."

Her words rang true. I gave her a nod of agreement and reclined, letting my weight press her into the chair.

5

I have long believed that total honesty is ultimately self-serving. If you betray your lover and feel that confessing is the honorable course, you may go to bed with a clear conscience while your lover is left in ruins. To spare them the torment of truth, one might choose silence or even deception. Likewise, to shield yourself from the pain of harsh realities, you either lie to yourself or reshape the truth to your convenience.

How does memory function? How does it select the things that are memorable and worth keeping while discarding those that are not? Why do I remember an insignificant detail like the size of Kylie's shoes but forget my mother's birthday? I don't know.

How true have I been to myself in penning these lines? I am unsure. Have I misunderstood a glance or misjudged a gesture? Did I misconstrue a signal? How far did my delusions extend? After all, isn't love itself a delusion? I'm not sure. I am aware of selective memory loss as a phenomenon, but what memory did I opt to forget? I have no clue. The reliability of these memories will forever be questionable. Did I reshape the truth to spare myself humiliation? Perhaps, but we'll never know.

Kundera once wrote, "Even the greatest love ends up as a skeleton of feeble memories." If I didn't believe in the grandeur of our love, I wouldn't find it worthy of narration. However, the fear of our love having an expiration date took root in the darkest recesses of my heart, growing alongside my love for Kylie. It served as a constant reminder that like all living things, our love would bloom, flourish, and eventually wilt, dying into mere memories.

The history of civilization is a chronicle of taming the penis. I had failed taming my penis and I knew I had to pay a high price for the consequences. The dread of imminent suffering often surpasses the suffering itself. A spark had ignited the flame, and I was aware that it would soon consume me. The name 'Jeff' was but a fleeting thought, yet it began to linger in my mind. I was certain this wouldn't end well. It always began this way – a spark that would erupt into an all-consuming inferno, an obsession so powerful that the need to rid myself of it would transform me into a murderer once again. So, I did my best to avoid broaching the subject, refrained from asking about him, and tried to convince myself that he no longer had a place in Kylie's life.

Our love was intoxicating, and my creativity had scaled unprecedented heights. I was in a state of unrivaled bliss, but the fear of imminent pain constantly cast its dark shadow over my joy. Was it merely the ghost of Jeff haunting me? Certainly not. It was the fear of inevitable loss – the understanding that all good things must eventually cease to be. Our love, too, was destined to exhaust itself, to reduce to a heap of ashes. I was acutely aware that the odds were stacked against our relationship. The anxiety stemming from the dread of losing Kylie was steadily eroding me. Each day, I told myself I needed to have a talk with Kylie and conclude our relationship. Yet after each encounter, it was evident that we were digging ourselves deeper into a hole from which escape seemed increasingly improbable.

Kylie had texted me early in the morning to tell me that she was going to be late. I had been working all morning and was thinking about food when Harry walked in. "Tell me you haven't eaten yet," he said, making a theatrical entrance.

I was genuinely happy to see him, so I stopped working and took him to Hagop's Kitchen, which, once again, I found myself visiting a few times a week, with Kylie.

"Where's Kylie?" asked Jack, seating us at my usual table.

"Yes, where is Kylie?" Harry chimed in.

I told them she was going to come later in the afternoon. Harry gave an absent-minded nod as he unwrapped the utensils.

"What's wrong?"

Harry shrugged. "Nothing. I should ask you the same question. I haven't heard from you for almost three weeks. What's going on?"

"Nothing."

"How are things with Kylie?"

"Good."

"You finally did it, didn't you? I can't believe you finally fell head over heels."

I was about to deny it but realized that would be futile, so I wistfully nodded.

"You're such an idiot! I told you, didn't I? Didn't I tell you this girl is going to be the end of you?"

"Why? Why are you saying that?"

"She's fucking half... not even half your age. How long is this going to last? I mean, she's not even your type..."

"What's my type?"

"I thought you would go for the other one, her friend... the blond toothpick."

"I think a type is someone you once loved and couldn't get enough of."

"Ah, shit. This is not good," Harry's face soured. "Does her mother know about this? She's going to kill you when she finds out."

It occurred to me that I hadn't even asked Kylie if she had talked about me to her mother. I assumed she hadn't, because if she had, I would have been aware of the consequences by now.

The young waitress brought some meze and disappeared. Harry was still steaming. "Seriously. What are you thinking? She's twenty-four fucking years old."

"Stop saying that!" I raised my voice. "Yes, she's twenty-four. So what? Why should I feel guilty because she's young?"

"Don't you feel like you're using her?"

"Using her? Who's using who? Did it occur to you that she might be using me? Besides, why is it necessary for one of us to be using the other? Have you ever thought about the fact that our age difference is giving another dimension to the relationship? We complement one another. She learns from my experience, and I learn from her curiosity."

"Tell me something. Would you have felt the same way if this girl was not as beautiful as she is?"

"Probably not, but that's completely irrelevant. Would you have eaten that morsel if it hadn't tasted as good as it does? Of course not. We love something because it's beautiful, it's charming, it tastes good, or whatever the fuck anything you love makes you feel."

Harry finished chewing, took a deep breath, and assumed his no-nonsense poise. "Listen, you know me too well. You know I'm not moralizing. I'm just worried about you, man. I've never seen you like this. What are you going to do when she moves on?"

I pretended to think about it. "What would I do if I get into an accident and die tomorrow? What would I do if I lost an arm? What would I do if my studio burned down?"

"Stop." Harry cut me off. "You know exactly what I'm talking about."

"What are you talking about?"

"I'm talking about the inevitable. There is no 'what if' here. Sooner or later Kylie is going to leave you. She's going to want a family, she's going to want children. Are you ready to marry her? A heartbreak at twenty-four is a migraine — it will pass in a few days — but a heartache at fifty-two is a fucking heart attack. It will kill you."

I thought of a million things to say, but I knew that none of them were convincing enough to be valid. After all, he was just vocalizing the silent warnings my mind had been whispering to me every single night. I took a gulp from my beer and told Harry what I would tell myself. "Harry, you have to understand. It's not just her beauty. It's her joie de vivre, it's her curiosity, her ability to ask all the right questions, her desire to probe, her sharpness. When she's with me she makes me feel that I am all that matters, and she's far more stimulating than most of my friends my age."

With a solemn sigh, Harry raised his eyebrows, clinked his beer bottle against mine, took a thoughtful sip, and let the flavor settle in his mouth before swallowing. "You know what? I'd probably do the same if I were you. Fuck it. Fuck me. Don't listen to me, man. Do your thing. Live your life." He raised his bottle one more time. "To life."

Harry had just left when Kylie walked in. She was in a festive mood and more talkative than usual, but my time with Harry had weighed heavily on my spirits. I had planned a small get-together for the evening, but now I was regretting it. I thought it best to address the situation with Kylie and consider ending our relationship, but I knew I needed to wait for the right moment to bring it up.

My right shoulder was in a lot of pain, and I had no desire to work. Kylie massaged it, applied an ice pack, then laid on the sofa with her feet on my lap and a book in her hand. A few minutes later, she suddenly slammed the book shut and asked, "So, what do you think has propelled your creativity the most?"

I shrugged.

"Come on, tell me." She nudged me with her feet.

"Picasso once said, 'I do not paint with my brush, I paint with my penis.' Years later, Norman Mailer paraphrased Picasso and said he doesn't write with his pen, he writes with his penis. I think all art is created by the penis."

"What if you don't have a penis?"

"Then you're in a tough spot. I don't envy female artists."

"Why is that?"

"For one, my art teacher Claude used to say, men have muses. The beauty, charm, and sensuality of the female body is far more inspiring than that of a male."

"I'm not sure if I agree with that," said Kylie, nudging me with her foot once again.

I felt a sudden wave of jealousy toward the man who would one day become Kylie's muse.

"Lisa, I mean... Kylie, look at you and look at me. Which one of us stirs more inspiration and creativity? Who embodies sensuality more, me or you?"

Kylie made a sour face and dismissed my argument.

"Also, compared to what you women can create, art is of no consequence."

"You mean having babies?"

"Absolutely. It's a lifelong project – a living form of art. As men, we're not capable of that. Maybe that's why we feel compelled to compensate by creating other forms of art."

"I really think sometimes you say things only for their shock value. Are you insinuating that men make better artists because they can't bear children?" Kylie's voice was filled with palpable disdain.

"Maybe. I'm not sure. It's something to think about, but what I'm saying is women have it tougher."

Kylie continued listening with a bitter expression on her face.

"I think all creativity is sexual or, at the very least, driven by sex. I know I'm ranting," I continued, "but sex offers physical validation, and art, in a way, provides existential validation. If you think about it, why else would you paint and then have an exhibition and invite people to come and see your work? It's a matter of acknowledgement. Like the existentialists say, you exist when your existence is acknowledged by the others. Your art exists when it is acknowledged by the others. Basically, what I'm saying is, 'I create, therefore I am.'"

Kylie stared at me intently. "You really are ranting. Something is off. What's wrong?"

It occurred to me that while I had been impatiently waiting to broach the subject, I had no idea what I was about to say. So, I took a deep breath and desperately attempted to articulate my thoughts. "Listen, Kylig, I've been thinking. I told you from day one... I knew this was going to happen. This is exactly what I was afraid of."

Kylie looked at me with a defensive smirk. "What exactly were you afraid of?"

"This. You... me... this."

"What's wrong with this?"

Here I was, supposedly trying to put an end to our relationship, and yet I was practically making love to her feet. "Kylig, I love women, but I have always managed to keep a safe distance from them. That's how I have survived all these years. I don't want to be the Timothy Treadwell of women."

"Who's Timothy Treadwell?"

"Treadwell was a man who loved bears. He spent years studying them in Alaska. He was utterly fascinated by them, until one day he was mauled and killed by one of them."

Kylie sheepishly smirked. "You think I will eat you?"

"Don't underestimate yourself."

"You're the one who's underestimating yourself. You're the big, bad wolf. I should be the one worrying about getting hurt."

"Darling, you might get hurt, but as Harry says, at your age you'll recover very fast. At my age there is no recovery. Trust me, I know what I'm talking about. All heartache comes from relationships. I'm not just talking about love. I'm talking about all kinds of relationships – mothers, daughters, fathers, sons, uncles, aunts, friends, acquaintances. In the end you always end up paying a price. Don't get me wrong, most of the time I'm glad to pay that price, but love is a different story. That's why love has always been equated with the sea. It's vast, it's beautiful, it's refreshing, it's deep, and it can easily drown you."

"Not when you're a good swimmer. And you know you are."

"A good swimmer knows when not to take a dive. Trust me. I think it was Lawrence Lovett who said it's great when love happens, but when human love starts out to lock individuals together, it courts disaster."

"Stop it already with your quotes. Fuck Lovett or whatever his name is. What the fuck does he know about love! I don't care what others think. And how the fuck do you remember all these quotes anyway?" Kylie scowled and pulled her feet away from my lap. "You know, you're like Frankenstein. Your brain is made of different parts of dead writers', artists', and philosophers' thoughts. Who created you?"

It's terrifying how love makes you relinquish so much power to the one you love. In one moment, they can give you complete bliss and euphoria, but in the next, they have the power to plunge you into utter misery.

I guess Kylie recognized the hurt in my eyes. "I was showing my work to some of my friends the other day, and one of them said my paintings are beginning to look like yours, and the others agreed."

"You're a master in avoiding emotional topics, aren't you?" I asked, a pitiful lilt coloring my voice.

"Why, what did I do?"

"You're telling me that you didn't even realize you completely swayed from what we were talking about?"

Kylie shrugged. "What do you want me to say? Why do you want to spoil a beautiful moment with a painful discussion like this?"

"Fine," I said, breaking the long silence. "What were you saying?"

"Nothing. Forget it."

"Come on, tell me."

"Nothing. I was just saying that everybody thinks I'm, like... copying you. And in a way, they're right. Your work is influencing mine."

"Why should that bother you? We're all influenced by someone in one way or another. Picasso once said, 'Good artists copy, great artists steal.' It's okay to copy – we all start out that way – but to be a great artist you have to take it in, process it, and make it your own. At this point all you need to do is paint. Don't worry about anything else. The more you paint, the closer you will get to finding your own language."

Kylie remained silent. I lit a cigarette and gave her a wink. "You're good. All you need to do is paint."

"I used to love what I was doing," Kylie murmured, her lips pulling into a pout. "But now, I don't even know.... I've become so critical of my work."

"That's a good sign. I think there are always four stages in creativity. The first stage is when you have no idea what you're doing, so you're fearless and you have a blast doing it. The second stage is when you know there are rules, so you're terrified and paralyzed. The third stage is when you know the rules and you can apply them and so you're good. But you will be fantastic only when you know the rules and you're confident enough to be able to break them. That's when you surpass yourself."

Kylie gave it some thought and exhaled. "Then I'm probably in stage two. I am constantly producing, but most of the time I'm terrified and not happy with the results."

"Producing... that's your problem. You're obsessed with output. The real key is to revel in the process of painting. Don't worry about stacking up paintings. Look at me. Why do you think I'm having trouble with my pieces? Because I'm trying too hard to produce. Every time I go to that wall with the intention of producing a new piece, I come out empty-handed. But when I start painting to just enjoy the process, I get pleasantly surprised. Forget the final product. The important thing is the process. Enjoy it. Go crazy and have fun with it."

"It's easy for you to say that," said Kylie pensively. "You have produced all that work and have made a name for yourself. You can afford to take your time and play. But me, I'm just starting and I feel that I have so much to prove..."

"Trust me, I understand. But this is exactly when you need to be in an open, playful mode in order to find the language you can express yourself best in."

We sat in silence for a minute, Kylie contemplating what I had just said, me taking in her carefree beauty and unassuming charm. It was already past – time for my friends to show up – so I bent over Kylie, kissed her forehead, and was about to go wash up when she took my hand. "Jules, did I do this? Did I seduce you?"

"I thought I did." I smiled.

"Maybe we both did."

"I am the adult here," I said. "I should be able to stop this right now, before it's too late."

"You keep saying that," frowned Kylie. "I'm an adult too, and I'm asking you why? Why would you want to stop it?"

"Because it's not right. Because this love is like a bull in a china shop. Sooner or later, it's going to create a big mess."

"Look, I know this isn't the ideal makings of a relationship, and I know there's no future for us. But for me, it's all about embracing the present," Kylie asserted, stealing a puff from my cigarette. "And if it's the age thing... You need to know that when I look at you, I don't see an older man. I see an incredibly talented artist and a wonderful human being."

"Yes, but for how long?"

Kylie squeezed my hand. "Forever. When you think of Freud, do you think of this frail old man, or do you think of this brilliant psychiatrist? When you think of Matisse, do you think of him as an old man, or you think of him as this master painter? Talent, intellect, and character trump age anytime."

"You're a drug. You should come in pills or vials. I can smoke, swallow, inject, and inhale you anytime. As a matter of fact, I can see myself getting addicted to your high."

"Good. Because I am already addicted to you." She pulled me down and kissed me. "Don't go."

"People will start coming any minute."

"I don't care. I wish no one was coming." Kylie stopped kissing me and asked. "What's 'kiss' in French?"

"*Baiser.* Do you want to know what's 'kiss' in Armenian?" Kylie nodded.

"*Hampouyr.* Can you say it?"

Kylie did a perfect job imitating me.

"*Håm* in Armenian is 'taste,' and *pouyr* is 'smell.' So a hampouyr is a combination of 'taste' and 'smell.'"

"Hampouyr," Kylie repeated after me, savoring the sound in her mouth. "I like that."

As we continued kissing, I truly wished there was a way to dog-ear a day or at least a few hours.

6

Lucy is vivacious, plump, funny, and beautiful. She teaches literature at the Armenian Unified School in Glendale. I was twenty-three when I met her, shortly after moving to Los Angeles. Through one of my mother's acquaintances, I was hired to teach art to the kids. We instantly hit it off and became lifelong friends after a very brief failed romance. She is intent on saving me from myself and she treats me like one would treat a seriously handicapped person.

It's Saturday morning. She has brought me a couple of za'atar croissants from Glendale and now waits as I prepare the coffee. "Are you still writing?" she asks.

I nod in confirmation as I pour the coffees.

"Are you going to tell me what it's about?"

I smile and shake my head. I know she knows what I'm writing.

"Hagop Oshagan, my favorite literary critic, says love and tears are indistinguishable," she comments, tearing a piece from her croissant.

"True," I agree, contemplating how for someone like Oshagan, a survivor of the Armenian Genocide, life itself must feel inseparable from tears.

"So, are you going to let me read it?"

I nod again.

We sit in silence, thinking of things not to say. Lucy finally exhales deeply and shakes her head.

"What?" I ask, bracing myself in a defensive stance.

"Nothing."

"Come on, say it."

"What do you want me to say?"

"That I'm crazy, and that..."

"Look," Lucy cuts me off. "She's smart, she's beautiful, she can even be funny, but she's a manipulating bitch."

"How do you know?" I challenge, my voice raising slightly.

"Because I've met her," she counters with even more force. "She plays the perfect seductress – charming but tough, sexy but shy, strong but fragile. I can see how one can fall for her, but yes, I'm going to say it again, she is half your age, for fuck's sake, and if you think that's nothing, you're wrong."

"Let me ask you this," I say, trying to calm her down. "If you were having an affair with a twenty-five-year-old kid and told your friend Anne about it, what do you think she would say?"

Lucy scoffs, her face twisted in a sneer. "She'd probably say, 'Good for you, girl.'"

"And why can't you do the same for me? Is it because I'm a man?"

"Yes," Lucy fires back. "Well, no. If I told Anne I was head over heels for a twenty-five-year-old, and it was making me miserable, she'd tell me I was out of my mind! A fling is one thing, but contemplating a future together? She'd tell me that's madness."

She's probably right. I'd say the same thing to her, so I bite my tongue and shake my head. Lucy can't stand silence.

"You know what? Fuck you," she exclaims, exasperated, as she bangs her coffee mug on the table. "You're not even trying. You want to wallow, then go ahead and fucking wallow! So, you're unhappy. Boo-hoo. Who the fuck is happy these days? Drown in your self-pity. I've had enough!" She pushes her half-eaten croissant away. Standing up abruptly, she catches my contrite gaze, sighs, then pulls her chair closer and sits back down. "Jules, you can't do this to yourself. You have to shake this off. Get outside, enjoy the sun, take long walks…. You live in Venice, for heaven's sake. Walk the canals, stroll along the beach. If you want to write, then write, but do it outside, at a coffee shop."

I tell her that I am walking every day.

"Not enough. I want to hear you say it. Say, 'I will spend more time outdoors.'"

I say it.

For years, Roland had been promising me an exhibition at his friend's gallery in Paris. Now that my recent show in Los Angeles was what he termed a success, an exhibition at Galerie Nave seemed more probable than ever.

"It's a done deal," Roland said when I visited him at his gallery. "The date hasn't been confirmed yet, but I'd say you have a little over a year to prepare. I suggest you start now, because after your recent sales, you've practically no pieces left for the Paris show."

He was right. His gallery had sold thirty-three of my works, two were on hold, and Roland wanted to retain the remaining seven in case collectors returned for more.

During my last visit to Paris, I had attended an opening at Galerie Nave. I was impressed by the quality of art on display and the crowd it had drawn. The thought of finally exhibiting in my hometown filled me with excitement, and when I shared the news with Kylie, she was overjoyed. "I'm coming with you," she declared, showering me with kisses.

"What makes you think I'll take you with me?"

"I don't care. I'm coming, whether you like it or not." She continued to pepper my face with kisses. "Meanwhile, you're going to teach me French. Promise me. Promise?"

I promised.

Kylie's enthusiasm was infectious. This would be her first trip abroad, and I could think of nothing more thrilling than sharing my Paris with her – wandering the streets hand in hand, sipping coffee at Le Deux Magots, exploring Musée d'Orsay, and enjoying croissants at Boulangerie Migneaux, not far from where my mother lived. But dealing with my mother was a different matter. Having lost my father at a young age, she had morphed into a clingy, overbearing figure who desperately sought in her sons all the roles she had lost – father, husband, lover – failing to understand that the sum of two little boys does not come to one adult man. We've always had a strained relationship, and even after almost thirty years, she hasn't forgiven me for escaping her control and moving to Los Angeles. In her view, a serious artist would never abandon Paris for a culturally deprived city like L.A. Moreover, I knew she was still upset because during my last two visits I had declined to stay with her and her two elderly dogs in her cramped two-bedroom apartment on Rue Didot in the fourteenth arrondissement. Despite my brother's and my best efforts to convince her to move, she had adamantly refused, even though navigating the stairs to her fourth-floor apartment was increasingly challenging for her.

"So did you call your friend about a show for me?" asked Kylie, lying next to me on the divan while I took a break from painting.

"I did," I said, following the contour of her profile with my index. "I showed him four pictures. He liked them, but honestly, I don't think you're ready for an exhibition."

Kylie frowned and turned away.

"Not for a solo show," I continued. "Start with group shows. Paint enough works so that you have a bulk to choose from. There is such a thing called living with your art. You have to live with them, see them every day, then make up your mind. Sometimes a work you don't initially like will grow on you over time, while other times a piece you're initially drawn to will lose its appeal, making you realize it doesn't satisfy you."

"Well, I showed some of my works to a gallery on La Cienega, and the man told me to call him in a few months, that he might be able to fit me in a group show."

"That's wonderful."

Kylie nodded, rested her palm on my face, and kissed me. "I have to go. There's something wrong with Picasso's tail. For some reason he's shedding. I need to take him to the vet."

I kissed her back.

"That's it. From now on, no more cats for me," she said, keeping her hand stuck to my face. "Have you ever thought about what it would be like to have a tail?"

"It's funny you say that," I said. "Hermann Hesse in *Rosshalde* says we artists paint because we don't have tails like intelligent animals who are capable of expressing all the nuances of their emotions with their tails."

"That would be awesome. I would have loved to have a long, beautiful tail. I think about that all the time. For a while, I was obsessed with the idea. Wouldn't it be fascinating? Imagine having a tail like a horse, right here where your spine ends. You could trim it, braid it, or style it however you wanted. It would be so graceful. Imagine, you're sleeping next to me, naked, and I could caress your body with my tail. There would be a whole culture about it. An entire industry would be based on tails. There would be shampoos, conditioners, and even specific combs and brushes designed for tails. There would be tail-related accidents. Your tail might get stuck in a car door, or you might start losing hair from it, like Picasso."

"You might go crazy like Van Gogh and cut your own tail," I chimed in, biting her shoulder.

Kylie grimaced in pain, then bit my hand. "People might even have cosmetic surgery performed on their tails."

"Yes, there would be old sayings about tails, like 'She who steps on other people's tails keeps her tail tucked in,' or 'Keep your tail to yourself.' And if you have a fight with your mother, and you regret it, you go back home literary with your tail between your legs."

"I like that." Kylie laughed. "I was reading something the other day about this guy who says he was abducted by aliens. He says they had short tails like Dobermans do."

"Dobermans are not born like that. That's how they get after surgery." I pushed the tress of hair away from her face and admired her beauty, wishing she had some imperfection… anything that would make it easy for me to contain my love for her.

"What?" she asked.

"Nothing."

"So do you think there's intelligent life out there?"

I continued watching her, mesmerized.

"Hello? Where are you? You were here a minute ago."

"I'm watching your lips move, but I can't hear anything. I get enthralled by the beauty of your lips, your eyes, your nose, and everything else becomes a distraction. All I want to do is to kiss you."

She smiled and shook her head. "You never listen to me. I'm serious. Do you think there's intelligent life out there?"

"There better be, because there sure is no intelligent life down here. If we're the only ones and this entire universe is entrusted to us, then we're seriously fucked," I said, lighting a cigarette.

"I'm sure there is. I bet you if one day a space shuttle we send passes by an inhabited planet out there, they would have a shit attack. They'd go, 'Oh shit, turn off the lights, don't let those idiots see us.'" Kylie laughed and glanced at her buzzing phone.

I couldn't help but peek and notice Jeff's name on the screen. A wave of revulsion went through me. Kylie sat up, snatched the cigarette from my fingers, and tossed it in an empty beer can. "By the way, my parents want to invite you over."

"You, or your parents?"

"What do you mean?"

"Was it your idea or your mom's?" I asked with an unnerved tone in my voice.

"What difference does it make?" replied Kylie, genuinely confused.

"Was it your mother's idea to invite me?"

"I suggested to her that we should invite you over, and she agreed. I was thinking you could come over next Tuesday. Why are you upset?"

"I'm upset because it's going to be a very uncomfortable situation," I almost yelled. "I really don't feel like sitting at a table with your mom and dad. I don't think I can come."

"Fine, then don't come," said Kylie, getting up. "I have to go before the vet closes." She grabbed her bag, gave a quick peck on my cheek, and ran out yelling, "I'll see you tomorrow."

Seeing Jeff's name on Kylie's phone really killed my mood. It suddenly occurred to me that she was about to meet Jeff. I had no doubt that taking Picasso to the vet was on her agenda, but somehow, I believed that Jeff was also in the plan. Within the past three weeks I had come to believe in the inevitability of a breakup. It would be naive to believe that Kylie and I would spend the rest of our lives together. And so I realized that I had begun to look for reasons, or even create reasons, to reach the inevitable as soon as possible. For months now I had been trying my best to prepare for the fateful day to come.

I drank myself to stupor and had just fallen asleep when I was awakened by a knock on the door. At first, I tried to ignore it, thinking it might be a vagrant, but after a few more knocks, I got up, looked through the peephole, and recognized Harry's pale face in the dim light. Deeply troubled, I opened the door and let him in. "What are you doing here? Are you okay?"

"Sorry, Jules. Were you sleeping?" Harry asked, walking in and scanning the room with an uncharacteristically serene look in his eyes. "Are you alone?"

"Yes. What's going on?"

"Nothing. I couldn't sleep. I needed to get out of the house."

"And you drove all the way here? What's bothering you?"

Harry sat in his usual chair, at the table, and kept silent. I poured myself a glass of cold water and sat facing him. He took a sip from my water, then looked at his watch. "Listen, I need to ask you something."

"What is it?"

Another long silence. "Jules, would you say I was a positive influence in your life?"

"What kind of question is that? Of course."

"Would you say I somehow enriched your life?"

"Harry, man, what the fuck are you talking about? How can you even ask that?"

"Just tell me, yes or no?"

"Of course you have. You have no fucking idea how much I love you, man. Is this why you drove all the way here?"

Harry absentmindedly nodded and, after a brief silence, stood up.

"What's going on, Harry?"

"Nothing. For the past thirty years, I've forced myself to paint because that's the one thing I believed I was good at. But I'm done creating fucking commodities. All this talk about art being noble and profound feels like such a farce now. I think I've made the right decision. It's all good."

"What decision? What are you talking about?"

Harry shrugged. "I should head out. It's all good." He smiled, pulled me into a long embrace, kissed my cheeks, and walked out.

"Why don't you spend the night here?" I yelled after him.

He either didn't hear or simply ignored me, slamming the door behind him.

I did not hear from Harry for five days, even though I had left him half a dozen messages. I also did not hear from Kylie all weekend, but I forced myself not to call or text her. On Monday, around noon, she showed up looking tired and under the weather. She said she had not left the house for three days and had bad period cramps. We had lunch, then attempted to do some work, but eventually gave up on the idea.

"Let's go out on a walk," said Kylie. "Let's go to the canals. We both need some fresh air."

Sure enough, the bright sun and the fresh air lifted our spirits. On our way back, when we stopped at Tony's for a cup of coffee, Kylie asked, "So, you're coming over tomorrow, right?"

"What's tomorrow?"

"Our place. I told Mom you're coming."

I had never agreed to go, but after some thought, I had decided to accept the invitation to satisfy my curiosity and appease her at the same time.

"You are?" said Kylie, excited when she realized I did not categorically object.

I smiled.

She kissed me, elated, and was about to take her first sip of coffee when my phone rang. It was an unknown number, and I had no intention of answering it, but Kylie automatically picked up the phone and playfully answered, "*Alo, oui?*"

A second later, with a stern look on her face, she extended the phone to me. "It's Harry's brother."

I had met Alex only once, a few years ago, at their mother's funeral. I knew he lived in Toronto and would visit his mother and brother every other year, but I also knew that Harry was not very fond of him.

"Hello?" I said, with a tight feeling in my stomach.

A somber, hoarse voice answered. "Yes, this is Alex. I am sorry if I'm bothering you, but I'm afraid I have some bad news. I know my brother was a good friend of yours, and my daughter, Zoe, says he always talked about you…" Alex stopped, probably expecting me to brace for the blow, then continued. "Yes, so I am sorry to say that Harry passed last week."

"How?" I managed to ask after a long silence.

"Yes, he… committed suicide on Thursday morning."

"Thursday morning?"

"Yes, sometime very early in the morning. He took a whole bottle of sleeping pills and then hung himself in the garage."

I struggled to believe what I was hearing. "What garage? Where?"

"Well, apparently he did it downstairs, in the parking space of his apartment."

I groped for words and came up with an unfamiliar grunt.

"Yes, so he left a letter, asking to be cremated, which we already did. But he also has mentioned that he wants you to have some of his paints and brushes. And he has a bunch of art books that you might want."

"Thank you," I muttered.

"We'll, I'll be leaving tomorrow morning, going back to Toronto, but my daughter is staying a few more days to take care of everything. I'm going to text you her number so you can call her and go pick things up."

"Okay…"

"Yes, so… then take care, and again, I am very sorry for the bad news." Alex's voice broke. He hung up.

With a look of utter disbelief in her eyes, Kylie held my hand, kissed it, then sat with me in deafening silence.

Harry's death destroyed me. I knew I couldn't have had anything to do with what had happened – but recognizing I was probably the last person he saw, and had not foreseen his action or read his state of mind, diminished whatever sleep I was eking out at nights.

A week later, stepping into Harry's apartment amplified my guilt and sent a wave of debilitating sadness through me. I had not been in his apartment for at least seven years

— seven years of me assuring him that one of these days I would visit him and take a look at his recent paintings.

It was obvious that his niece, whose name had slipped my mind, had been crying. She was lanky, with a boyish figure, almost no breasts, and appeared to be in her midthirties. She shook hands with Kylie and me, attempted to smile, and led us inside. Kylie followed me, intently surveying the apartment, flabbergasted by the assault of the brilliant colors emanating from the paintings on the walls.

The living room was unkempt and smelled of popcorn in an old movie theater. The tan carpet was covered with paint blotches and stains, and the state of the furniture made it obvious that Harry had left everything intact after the death of his mother. The bedroom was full of hundreds of paintings, some stretched, others rolled up, leaving a narrow isle around the neatly made bed. Almost all the paintings were portraits, beautiful yet disturbing, some reminiscent of Modigliani, others of Matisse, painted with raw, vivid colors and confident brushstrokes.

"I think we're going to keep the paintings, but you can have a few of them, if you see something you like. Also, my dad said you can have all the paints and the brushes. We have some cardboard boxes here you can use," said the niece, wiping her cheeks. Her dark, almond eyes glittered in the hazy sunlight seeping through the window, and she looked far more charming than my first impression of her.

The room Harry painted in was also full of paintings, with plastic containers, cans, tubes of paint, and brushes scattered all over the room. There was a brand-new white canvas on the easel, and the smell of acrylic paint gone bad made it impossible to breathe.

I told Kylie to fill a couple of boxes with paints and brushes, while I began to fill another box for myself.

"He really loved you, you know," the niece almost whispered, leaning against the doorframe. "He always talked about you. I was planning on visiting him two weeks ago, but... last-minute change of plans. I wish I had."

"What are you going to do with the paintings?" I asked after a long silence.

"I don't know. My father says maybe we'll have an exhibition in Toronto. I think I will rent one of those big vans and drive all these home. Also, there are boxes of photos and letters that I want to keep. The rest of the stuff goes to the Starvation Army."

"You mean the Salvation Army."

"Right, that's what I meant."

"I still can't believe it," she sighed. "I could never imagine him doing something like that."

I gave her an abstract nod and stood up. It seemed to me that she was expecting me to say something, so I said, "You know, Michel Foucault says there is not a piece of conduct more beautiful or, consequently, more worthy of careful thought than suicide. One should work on one's suicide throughout one's life."

The niece contemplated that for a moment. "Well, you can't consider suicide throughout your life if you end your life prematurely. But then again, I suppose that's the whole point."

Kylie also stood up. "Is it okay if I take these two boxes?" She pointed at the boxes full of paint and brushes.

"Sure. You can take more if you like. Anything you want."

Kylie threw in a few more tubes and a small sketch pad and, after lingering a few more minutes, she shot a pleading look at me.

The niece helped us carry the boxes and a few paintings to the car and promised to call us if she needed anything before leaving for Toronto.

On our way back, Kylie wouldn't let go of my hand.

"Maybe he did the right thing," I said, probably to evoke an emotional response.

Kylie pressed her fingernails in my palms. "I'll kill you if you die on me."

There was a long moment of awkward silence when Lisa opened the door. We hadn't seen each other for years, and time had turned her into a mature woman. It seemed she had embraced her fifty years, opting for comfort over style yet preserving her natural beauty and gaining a motherly quality in her appearance. She was in baggy pants, an oversize T-shirt, and a pair of tan sandals. Was it her way of letting me know that I wasn't important enough to dress up for? Perhaps, but it wasn't enough to offend my sense of aesthetics.

We shook hands, smiled; she intently examined my smile, probably recognizing my desperate attempt to be at ease, then gave me a perfunctory kiss on the cheek and walked me inside.

The house was nothing like I had imagined. Except for the books there was not much that would remind me of the chaotic Lisa I had once known. The furniture was mostly midcentury, comfortable and unassuming, and everything was neatly arranged, with no trace of any of my paintings on the walls. Her husband, Larry, whom I had met few times years ago when they weren't married yet, was standing at the bar, talking on the phone. When he saw me, he apologetically waved and continued talking while Kylie came out of her room, gave me a quick hug, kissed my cheeks, and said, "I'm so glad this is finally happening."

"We might as well sit at the dining table," said Lisa, leading me to what I assumed was the dining room.

I had just taken a seat when Larry walked in beaming and extended his impressively large hand. "I'm so sorry, I've been on the phone for almost two hours. Supposedly I'm off today.... So, what are you drinking?"

"I got it," said Kylie, placing a glass of whiskey in front of me.

"I see you're still not drinking wine," observed Lisa, who was sitting next to me.

I shook my head, smiled, and turned to Larry. "Wine gives me headache."

"Bad wine gives me headache too. It's the sulfate. That's why we only drink organic wine. I don't think there's sulfate in this," said Larry, taking a sip from his wine.

"I'm sure there is," said Kylie. "Maybe less."

"Cheers," I said raising my glass.

"*Genats,*" Lisa chimed in.

"You remember. I'm impressed."

"What's that?" asked Kylie.

"That's how you toast in Armenian," explained Lisa.

"To Kylie, for bringing us together," I continued, and clinked glassed with the three of them.

"You're supposed to make eye contact while toasting, otherwise it's seven years of bad sex," said Kylie to her mother, laughing.

Lisa shot a scolding look at her daughter.

"Dig in," said Larry, and he began to eat.

I was about to thank Lisa for remembering my culinary preferences – the boeuf bourguignon served with mashed potatoes – but chose to hold my tongue instead.

"So, Kylie tells me you're an emergency doctor," I said to break the uncomfortable silence after a while.

"Guilty as charged."

"It must be pretty crazy, huh?"

"It is." Larry wiped his mouth with a napkin. "This morning I was thinking, 'I'm too old for this,' even though I've always loved the excitement that comes with it."

"Why? What happened this morning?" asked Kylie.

"Nothing specific. The usual insanity. They brought in this man who had completely lost it. Imagine, he goes into his neighbors' backyard and starts cutting down their trees because he thinks the trees are crossing the fence and coming into his backyard for water, at night."

"Trees? Are you serious?" Kylie let out an exaggerated laugh.

"Trees," stressed Larry. "His neighbor tries to stop him, so he runs after his neighbor with his chainsaw and falls, sawing off his own leg."

"His entire leg?" asked Kylie.

"Well, his leg was dangling. He had lost so much blood," explained Larry.

"Larry, please, we're eating," rebuked Lisa, looking at me apologetically.

"That's okay. Really," I assured her.

"Is he alive?" Kylie pressed.

"He is, but he lost at least forty pounds in one day."

"Forty pounds, how?"

"Well, we had to amputate his leg," said Larry, winking at me.

"Dad!" Kylie laughed, boxing her father in the arm.

I joined in the laughter.

Lisa took a sip from her wine and turned to me. "I'm sorry about Harry. Kylie told me. I was shocked."

I shook my head.

"The last person you would expect…" continued Lisa.

"He was such a good guy."

"Yeah, sorry about that," Larry said solemnly. "I hear he was one of your best friends."

"Yes, he was, and I feel horrible because I didn't see it coming."

"You can't feel guilty," said Larry. "I see it all the time... attempted suicides. It's usually a snap decision. It's not even a decision.... It's a matter of minutes. The more you think about it, the less the probability of doing it. My uncle committed suicide when I was twelve. Not even his wife, my aunt, could believe he would do a thing like that. People do it because they reach the limit of their tolerance. Once it gets there, nothing matters – wife, children, parents, nothing. You want to end life, and the only way to end it is by death."

"I don't think the opposite of life is death. I think the opposite of life is what Emerson called 'quiet desperation.' When you're dead inside and you go through the motions. The world is full of people who exist in a state that's the opposite of life," said Kylie.

Lisa measured her daughter with a look of concealed surprise.

"Well, think of it this way," said Larry, trying to interject some levity into the conversation. "Your friend is in good company: Van Gogh, Ernest Hemingway... who else... Robin Williams..."

"Mark Rothko, Diane Arbus..." added Lisa.

"Don't forget Kurt Cobain and David Foster Wallace," chimed in Kylie.

"Didn't Gorky commit suicide too?" asked Lisa to no one in particular.

"Who's Gorky?" asked Larry.

"Arshile Gorky, Armenian artist. Used to be one of his favorites." Lisa turned to me. "Right?"

I nodded.

"Can we talk about something more pleasant?" Kylie said, reaching for her wineglass. "To life. What was it again? *Gentas?*"

"*Genats*," I corrected.

Lisa remained silent during the rest of the dinner. I could sense her nervous energy every time Kylie refilled my glass, offered some more bread, or laughed at something I said; the kind of exaggerated laughter reserved only to appease a lover. I was hopping Kylie would scale back her attention to me, but on the contrary, it appeared to me that she was trying her best to make it obvious that there was something more than meets the eye between us.

After dinner, while we were moving from the dining room to the living room, Kylie tugged my arm. "Do you want to see my room? Come, I'll show you," she proposed, dragging me to her room. As soon as she nudged the door nearly shut with her foot, she began to kiss me.

"What are you doing? Are you crazy?" I panicked.

Her face flushed, she continued to press her lips to mine. "I need you," she murmured, a note of desperation creeping into her voice.

"Stop. The fucking door is open."

"I don't care," whispered Kylie in my ear, thrusting her hand in my pants and grabbing hold of my cock, which had already been burning in my pants.

"Stop it. Your mother might walk in any minute," I said, pushing her away and trying to get out.

She bit my lip, let go of my cock, and waited for me to regain my poise.

As I stepped into the living room, Larry swiftly pocketed his phone, greeted me with a warm smile, and gestured toward the sofa.

"So," I started, settling onto the sofa opposite him, "you must have some stories. Emergency rooms... I can only imagine..."

"Well," Larry began, his face showing a hint of weariness, "it's crazy. The regulars are the most exhausting."

"Regulars?"

"Yes. There are a bunch of them who are there a few times a week. Drug addicts, mostly. And then there are the ones who have serious issues. Like this young Hispanic guy who shows up almost every week after swallowing something."

"Swallowing? Like what?"

"You'd be surprised. Just a few days ago, he came in with a spoon lodged in his esophagus."

"A spoon?"

"A teaspoon. It's a condition. I've seen people swallow pencils, coins, all kind of things... even a vibrator."

Lisa entered, balancing coffee and dessert on a tray. It'd been a while since I'd last been a guest in someone's house. Larry was extraordinarily congenial and affable, but Lisa remained quiet throughout the evening, keeping track of the conversation and studying me with an intense gaze. She had never been one for small talk, and she seemed even more reticent and pensive now.

"So, what do you think?" Larry asked as I stood up to leave. "Is my girl as talented as I think she is?"

"Dad!" Kylie protested, playfully punching her father in the arm. "What are you expecting him to say? Don't put him in a predicament."

"She's incredibly talented," I assured him. "Seriously. She's very good."

"Well, thank you for guiding her. I don't know much about art, but I can see a clear progress in her work."

"That's true," Lisa agreed, sounding somewhat reluctant. "There is significant improvement."

"Good to hear," I responded, shaking hands with Larry at the door.

Lisa gave my cheeks a quick peck and retreated indoors, while Kylie accompanied me to my car.

"Thanks for coming, Julig," she said, enveloping me in a hug. "I love you so much."

"I love you more," I responded, kissing her. As I turned back one more time to wave goodbye, I was sure I saw Lisa's silhouette by the door.

7

It's late afternoon, and I'm spray-painting a metal rack in my driveway when I spot my neighbor Derek striding toward me, arms folded across his chest and a congenial smile playing on his lips. He murmurs something incomprehensible, compelling me to halt my work and remove my mask.

"It's getting a little nippy," he comments. I can't help but notice how his bushy beard seems too imposing for his slender, short stature. I consider asking if he has a permit for that beard. I think some people do not deserve the attention and the gravity that a beard bestows upon them.

"Hello, Derek."

"They broke into my car again last night," he sighs, shaking his head with a tinge of bitterness. "That's twice in the past six months."

"Sorry to hear that, Derek."

"Did you happen to hear anything out of the ordinary? I can't understand why the darn alarm didn't go off."

"What did they steal?"

"Not much. They just smashed the window and nabbed my jacket and my gym bag, which was almost empty."

I offer him my most sympathetic nod.

"The neighborhood is going downhill quickly. Just two days ago, my girlfriend had a scare when she spotted a homeless guy peering in through the kitchen window."

I feign shock and express my concerns about the need for increased vigilance.

Derek agrees and shares his intentions to start a petition for the installation of streetlights on our block, to which I assure him of my support.

"So, how's Kylie?" he asks unexpectedly. "I haven't seen her around for a while."

"She's good, just swamped with work."

"Tell her Derek from the coffee shop said hi."

I promise him that I will relay the message. He lingers for a few more minutes before finally leaving. I return to my task, finish spray-painting the rack, and leave it outside to dry before heading in to resume writing.

A few days after our visit to Kylie's parents, I accompanied Kylie on a shopping trip. We found two elegant black dresses, a leather jacket, and a pair of rugged boots. On our way home, while having coffee at Tony's, a bohemian-looking woman in her midforties with long blond hair, wearing a long, flowy dress and a wrist full of bracelets and carrying an oversize tote bag, sauntered by. She shot a sideways glance in my direction, then made an abrupt detour toward our table.

"Hello, would you like me to read your palm?" she meowed with a thick Eastern European accent. "I will do this for free," she added, flashing a charming smile as she held out a hand.

Kylie looked at me, laughed, and – seeing my hesitation – urged me to give the woman my hand.

"Christ, you're painfully beautiful. How can I resist!" I jested, pulling out a chair for her before extending my hand. She traced the lines of my palm with her slender fingers, exchanged a smile with Kylie, and began the reading. "You are not from here," she mused. "You are from somewhere in Europe, maybe Germany or France. I think maybe Paris."

Kylie and I exchanged looks of bewilderment.

"You are an artist. May be a musician or a painter," she continued.

"Okay," I chuckled, considering that such a guess wouldn't be too challenging given my appearance.

Detecting my sarcasm, the woman shook her head. "Okay. You love women and you have many women friends but are afraid of... how you say..." she finally found the word "commitment." She then scrutinized my palm even more closely. "I think maybe your name is Julian."

I attempted to withdraw my hand, but instead of releasing it, she planted a kiss on my palm and burst into laughter, exclaiming in a strong Italian accent, "Julian, it's me, Paola!"

We both rose instantly, embracing each other. Paola planted a long, wet kiss on my lips, then turned to Kylie. "I am sorry for this, but I have not seen this man for more than ten years." She then introduced herself to Kylie with a kiss on each cheek. "I am Paola."

"That was good, Paola. That was very impressive. Brava," I complimented, keeping her in my arms.

"I knew you would not recognize me. So, you like my Polish accent?"

"I'm not sure if it was Polish, but it was good. I'm impressed."

Paola turned to Kylie. "When we met, I had very short orange hair. I was like a punk. I had just come from Rome to be a singer."

"Why are you back in L.A.?" I asked, once we had retaken our seats.

"I am here for work. I still live in Rome. I work for a clothing company."

"That's wonderful," I responded, genuinely delighted.

We spent over an hour reminiscing about the time

she spent in Venice, mostly in my company. We exchanged contact information and pledged to meet again. After she left, I sensed a trace of jealousy clouding Kylie's mood.

"*Mon dieu*, you are painfully beautiful," Kylie teased, mimicking my earlier comment. "But she really was gorgeous. Are you going to see her again?"

"I don't know. Maybe."

"You should," she suggested, although her tone suggested I shouldn't.

Back at home, Kylie treated me to a private fashion show, parading around in the dresses we had just bought. She had just curled up beside me for a short nap when my brother called. "Are you home?"

"Why, are you coming?" I asked jokingly.

"I wish. Why do you sound like that?"

"Like what?"

"I don't know. Different."

"I've been up all night."

"Why?"

"Too much on my mind."

"You're not alone, fucker."

"Yes, I'm not."

"I knew it. Did you hear what happened in Nice?"

"No, what happened?"

"Some guy drove a ten-ton cargo truck into a crowd celebrating Bastille Day. Remember two years ago when we were in Nice, we had beer with Maurice at the restaurant on Promenade des Anglais?"

"Yes. Okay?"

"Bullshit. I know you don't remember, but anyway, it happened right there, just across from that bistro."

"That's fucked up."

"Maurice called me. He said it was horrible. Some eighty people were killed."

"Any more uplifting news?" I asked sarcastically.

"Listen, I've been asking around about Gallery Nave."

"And?"

"I'm not sure if it's doing well. I talked to this guy who said he has worked with the gallery. He said it has been struggling. Apparently, the German partner has left, and they have been bleeding money. So, if I were you, I would think about it twice before committing to anything."

"So, what are you saying? I shouldn't do the show?"

"No, I'm just saying be careful with your dealings with them."

I closed my eyes and took a deep breath.

"*Alo?* Did you fall asleep?"

"No, I'm still here. How's *maman?*" This is a question I have always dreaded asking. Vahan has never made me feel guilty for leaving our mother's care to him, but I knew he had every right to resent me, and I dreaded the day he might voice his discontent.

"Maman is… maman. She's okay, I guess. I know she's excited about your visit, but of course she never shows it." Vahan then ranted about his son, Shant, my nephew, changing jobs and his ex-wife taking singing lessons at fifty-one before he hung up abruptly.

"Who was that?" Kylie asked, her voice heavy with sleep.

"My brother, Vahan," I replied, giving her a kiss and gently trying to extricate myself from the bed.

"Where are you going?" Kylie murmured, her fingers clutching mine. "You can't go."

"I know exactly what to do with the painting," I said, referring to the canvas I had been working on for the past two days.

"I want you," Kylie pleaded, her eyes brimming with desire.

"Again?"

"Yes, again. I never get enough of you." She looked flush and more youthful than ever.

"Why? Why do I love you so fucking much!" I exclaimed, pressing a kiss to her hand.

Kylie grinned and shrugged. "I don't know."

"What are you thinking about?"

"Nothing."

"You can't be thinking about nothing," I said. "It's impossible. It takes years of practice to be able to think about nothing."

"Is not thinking the same as thinking about nothing?" Kylie bit my palmar side.

"Good question."

Kylie took a deep breath and put my hand down. "I was thinking… After Harry's death… You know what you said about love being selfish and antisocial? I really don't want to stand between you and your friends."

"You're not," I assured her.

"Think about it. You haven't seen anyone for a while. Maybe we should invite them over."

"Tonight?" I asked.

"Why not?"

"I don't feel like seeing anyone. I want to be alone with you."

"This is exactly what I'm talking about. I think I'm making you antisocial."

"It's not you, Kylig. It's love. That's what love does. The moment two people lock, they close their social windows and doors and resign from the world. It's true, love *is* blind… blind not only to the shortcomings of one's lover, but to the world in general."

"I don't know if I agree with you. I think we see, but what we see becomes irrelevant, because our perception is tainted by love."

"What do you know about love? How many people have you loved?" This was purely rhetorical, a query whose answer I had always preferred to remain in the shadows.

"I know enough to recognize it." Kylie smiled and held my face in the palm of her hands. "Do you love me?"

"No, I'm crazy about you."

"Crazy enough to be committed?"

"I'm ready to spend the rest of my life in a loony bin."

"I'll move in with you and I'll never, ever leave your side."

"You're crazy!"

"No shit!" Kylie laughed, then solemnly met my gaze. "Were you in love with my mom?"

"Yes, of course I was. We were madly in love."

"What happened."

"Jesus, Kylig, we've been through this so many times."

"I want to know why you left her. Are you going to leave me, too?"

"Who said I left her?"

"Then what happened?"

"Nothing. I told you. We were too young. People shouldn't make life-altering decisions before they're twenty-five."

"Did my mom cheat on you?"

"Cheat? We both didn't believe in marriage and we both felt trapped. Were we cheating? It almost became a dare – who could do something more outrageous, more scandalous than the other?"

"Are you serious? My mom?"

"Our love was like a beautiful baby when it began, but we had no idea how to take care of it."

"So it died?" Her eyes were moist.

"I don't believe it died. Perhaps we gave it up for adoption."

"Was she still with you when she began her affair with my dad?"

I answered yes, and it struck me that the sad tone of my yes was merely to adhere to a protocol and service the drama.

Kylie took a deep breath. "I think I better head home. My room is a mess, and I need to do some laundry."

"And I believe I'm going to take a walk and then come back to work."

"Promise you're not going to drink."

I shook my head.

"Is that a yes or a no?"

"That's an 'I'll try.'"

"I don't like you when you drink. You become sloppy," said Kylie, assuming her no-nonsense attitude. "Besides, I want you alive."

"Who's dying? I have no intention of dying."

Kylie's eyes welled up. "I wouldn't know what to do if anything happened to you."

"Nothing is going to happen to me," I assured her.

"Do you love me?"

I kissed her and inhaled her breath.

"How much do you love me?" she asked, continuing our cross-questioning ritual that had become a daily practice.

"Enough to escape from the loony bin, fly to Paris, and bring you a salmon salad from my favorite restaurant, Café du Musée in Le Marais. And you?"

"Enough to run through the corridors of the loony bin yelling 'Fire, fire' at two o'clock in the morning. And when people wake up and ask me where the fire is, I'll tell them my heart is on fire. And you?"

"Enough to celebrate your birthday every single night and drive everyone even crazier."

"And I would act surprised every single night." Kylie burst into laughter.

"I love you so much that I'm jealous of you, because you get to spend all your time with yourself. Every minute spent without you, I consider it wasted. I live in you. I live for you. Because of you, I have become bipolar."

"Why bipolar? Why do you say that?" Kylie asked, confused.

"Because when I don't see or hear from you my world becomes bleak and dark. But the moment I catch sight of you, everything brightens up. I feel giddy and rejuvenated," I explained.

Wiping a teardrop rolling down her cheek, Kylie flashed a grin. "Really? I feel the same way. No matter who I'm with or what I'm talking about, I have to mention your name. I suddenly find myself talking about you."

"This is not good for either of us," I warned. "One's happiness should never be dependent on another person. Never." I kissed her lips, her eyes, her forehead, and got up.

"Promise you will never leave me."

I promised.

"No matter what?"

I reiterated my promise.

When I returned from my meeting with Roland, I assumed Kylie had departed, but then a muffled voice from the bathroom caught my attention. From my position by the bathroom door, I discerned that Kylie was conversing with her friend Luna over the phone. "No, that's not why

I'm not coming," I heard Kylie say in a slightly agitated voice. "No. Well, yes, I do love spending time with him..." Silence. "Because... Yes, I love him, and no, you're wrong. This is nothing like it was with Paul." Another momentary silence ensued, followed by the toilet flushing. "Yes, I know I'm crazy, and yes, I do see myself having kids with him. Yes, seriously." A prolonged silence. "I don't know, maybe somewhere south of France, Spain, Thailand... anywhere." Another silence. "No, I can't. Not tonight. Love you too."

The sound of the faucet ceased, and I sensed Kylie moving. I quickly stepped back to the doorway, feigning my arrival. As she emerged from the bathroom, I enfolded her in an embrace so tight it could potentially fracture a bone or two, and peppered her with kisses. My soul felt tickled. If I'd had any lingering doubts about Kylie's love for me, they had now evaporated completely. Her admission to Luna had me both elated and concerned about our relationship entering a serious phase.

Roughly an hour after Kylie had left, a knock on the door startled me. I opened the door and was taken aback to see Lisa's stern, grim face.

"Were you asleep?" she inquired as she stepped in.

"No, I was reading."

Lisa swept the entire studio with a glance, shaking her head, visibly impressed, then began to go through the stack of paintings leaning against the wall.

"I'm going to make myself a cup of coffee," I said, heading to the kitchen. "Would you like some?"

"No, thanks. If I have coffee now, I'll be up all night."

"That's probably why I couldn't sleep last night."

As Lisa cleared her throat with a small cough, a shiver of apprehension ran through me. I knew the conversation to follow wouldn't be pleasant, so I braced myself, poured two glasses of whiskey, and returned.

"There's a new vitality in your recent works. They exude a raw, unfinished energy," she observed, accepting one of the glasses from my hand. "Your previous works were more mature, less vibrant, more subtle and sophisticated, but these new pieces... They will sell, that's for sure."

Uncertain of what to say, I simply nodded and took a long sip from my whiskey. Lisa moved to the other stack of paintings near the door, casting a puzzled look at the pieces.

"Those are Kylie's..." I announced, a note of pride creeping into my voice. Lisa shook her head and fixed me with a sharp gaze. "I knew it. I knew this was going to happen. I warned her but she wouldn't listen to me."

"You're speaking as if she's dead."

"She's only twenty-five years old, for heaven's sake – just twenty-five. Do you have any idea what she's going through? She's aging right before my eyes."

"That's not called aging, Lisa, that's called growing up."

"She should be out with her friends, dancing, having fun, doing whatever the fuck people her age do these days. Instead, she's spending all her time here with you."

"What's wrong with that?" I tried not to raise my voice.

"What's wrong with that? How would you feel if she were your own daughter?"

"What are you talking about? There's nothing happening between us. She wanted to be a painter and I agreed to help her. That's all."

Lisa's expression turned incredulous. "Oh, please, Julian. Please. I know my daughter and I know what it's like to be in love. So, stop bullshitting. It's me you're talking to. Look at me."

It's baffling how easily a familiar rage, reserved only for a specific person, can resurface after decades of lying dormant.

"Listen to me," I fumed. "There's not one fucking kid out there who is capable of loving her as much as I do. She's an old soul and…"

"Fuck you, Julian. Old soul… Fuck you."

"She says she's bored to tears with kids her age. Talk to her. I didn't start this. God knows I tried to stay away."

"Enough, Julian. Just stop." Seeing Kylie's sneakers, Lisa shuddered, tightly clutching her handbag as she sat, pondering her next move.

"What do you want me to say, Lisa? Do you think I'm thrilled about this situation?" I asked in a near whisper.

"God. On my way here I was thinking maybe for once – after all these years – for once we could have a decent conversation, but obviously nothing has changed. Nothing. You're the same person you've always been, just thirty years older, which makes this even more deplorable. I was genuinely hoping that I could ask you to stay away from her, but it's useless. You're not going to stop." Lisa wiped her tears, bit her lower lip exactly the way Kylie does, then began to sob. "She's my baby. She's my little baby."

I gently put my hand on her shoulder and kissed her head. She shrugged off my hand and stood up. "I'm just wondering where you found the audacity to do something like this? You realize you're going to get hurt, right?"

I nodded solemnly.

"No, you don't understand." Lisa took a deep breath. "Ask her about Paul."

"Who's Paul?"

"Ask her. Let's see what she says. Ask her why the poor man was stalking her for months." Lisa grabbed her bag, walked to the door, then turned around. "I just hope you have an iota of dignity left in you to do the right thing. Just don't tell her I was here."

I kept mum about Lisa's visit when speaking with Kylie, even though I was dying to know the story behind Paul. Despite my eagerness to uncover the truth, I couldn't bring up his name without risking Kylie's suspicion. Resolute, I made the decision to end our relationship, irrespective of the potential fallout. My Paris exhibition loomed just two months away. The thought of shattering her anticipation for the trip gnawed at my conscience. She had been looking forward to it so eagerly, yet I knew it was essential to break things off beforehand. It was a tough decision, but it needed to be done.

Needless to say, my resolve to end it with Kylie intensified my love for her even more, and the idea of losing her turned me into a nervous wreck. I became more jealous, more possessive, and far more insecure. I found myself calling and texting her dozens of times a day, and when she was with me, my eyes were always fixed on her phone, checking every text she received. I tried to overhear every conversation she had and probe her mind on every decision she made.

I had spent most of the morning taking care of the shipping arrangements for my exhibition in Paris. I was physically tired but in an upbeat mood when I returned to my studio. Kylie was lying on the sofa, engrossed in her reading. I sat at her feet and kissed them.

"Here, finish it," Kylie said, shoving a half-eaten apple in my mouth.

I pushed the apple away.

"You know, it wouldn't really kill you if you tried eating something healthy every once in a while."

"I had one this morning."

"Bullshit. I brought you four apples and they are all still there."

"If an apple a day keeps the doctor away, will two apples a day keep two doctors away?"

"You know what? When I first met you, I thought, 'This man is a little crazy.' Now I know you are totally insane." Kylie chuckled, sticking her tongue out.

"What are you reading?"

"Milan Kundera's *Life Is Elsewhere*."

"Good choice. Did you already finish *Nausea*?"

"Of course. I finished it three days ago. I can't sleep at night, so all I do is read."

"What's keeping you up?"

"All kinds of things. Like the group show that's coming up. I hope I can sell some pieces. Sometimes it feels like I have put my life on hold. Like I have no idea what I'm doing with my life, what my next step is going to be.... Like, should I go back to finish graduate school?"

"What else?"

"Isn't that enough?"

"There's something else that's bugging you," I said, searching her eyes.

"You really want to know?"

"Of course I do."

Kylie reflected for a minute, then said, "My mom knows about us."

I did not respond.

"She knows for sure."

"How can you tell?"

"Last week she started fishing. She said we were acting like lovers at the dinner table."

"What did you say?"

"I told her there's nothing going on between us. Then she said she knows you too well."

"And?"

"She didn't push it. My dad didn't say anything but seemed a little upset. He just shook his head and walked away. Typical. He always does that when he's upset. He hates confrontation."

"I guess that's his way of coping with your mother."

Kylie made a disgruntled sound.

"I'm sorry. That was completely uncalled for," I conceded, lighting a cigarette. "Maybe you should stay away from me for a while. Sooner or later it's going to happen anyway."

"What do you mean?"

"How long do you think this love will last? Two years? Three years? How long do you think I will be able to turn you on? Eventually you will look at me and see an old man. You'll realize that I was only filling a void."

"So what? All love is the result of a need to fill some sort of a void."

"Besides, how long do you think you can keep Jeff on a leash?"

"I don't get it. So, what exactly are you implying?"

"I don't know what the fuck I'm saying. I'm just preparing myself for the inevitable hurt."

"You don't have to. I love you." Kylie's eyes turned moist. "Remember when you told me, 'Here, I'm giving you my heart on a platter. Please be careful with it. Don't trip and fall?'"

I gave a nod.

"I thought you did that because you trusted me. I didn't think you were going to constantly keep an eye on it to make sure I don't break it. How do you expect me not to trip and fall when you're constantly pushing me? I love you, you idiot.

I. Love. You." Kylie enunciated each word, punctuated by her fist against my chest. "Do you understand that? I love you so much, I wish everyone around me was you!"

"I love you too, Kylig, but I'm terrified. I'm scared because everything has a beginning, a middle, and an end. Right now, we're in the middle of it, but I know, sooner or later, there will be an end. Everything is born, grows up, and eventually dies. I guess that's why people have children. I had never thought about it that way, but it's true. A child is a continuation… a proof of that love. For the first time in my life, I want a child, but I know it's never going to happen."

"How do you know?" cried Kylie. "How the fuck do you know?"

"Because I won't allow it. I won't let you waste the prime of your life with me. Tomorrow, you will find a young, handsome man, fall head over heels, and look back and think how silly this entire episode was."

"Nobody will love me the way you do. Nobody. You've raised the bar so high, it will be impossible to love anyone after you. You're my everything. You made me who I am, you created me, then you fell in love with your own creation," Kylie fired back, her gaze piercing my soul. "I love you so much it feels like my heart will burst into smithereens. The only time I feel complete is when I am with you."

"Me too," I echoed. "And that's exactly why I think I should die right now, before it's too late. Right now, when our love is at its peak."

"Selfish asshole. You don't even care about the anguish you'll inflict."

"Of course I do, but there is something poetic and romantic about grieving the death of a loved one. You'll look stunning in a black dress, weeping over my grave behind dark glasses."

"You're an asshole."

"You don't understand. If I die now, or maybe in two years, you'd be in the prime of your life and you can have a fresh start. Time heals all wounds, Kylig. It might leave a scar, but it will make you sexier, and every time you look in the mirror that scar will remind you of your humanity."

"Fuck you," Kylie muttered, kicking me indiscriminately. "Fuck you."

I tried to restrain her by holding her feet, but she was strong enough to resist. I finally was able to hold her down and kiss her, but she bit my lip hard enough to draw blood. Sweaty, tearful, and salivating, we wrestled, bit, kissed, licked, slapped, and fucked until we were both spent, lying in the ashes of our extinguished passion.

With five weeks left before my exhibition in Paris, we were both filled with anticipation and impatience. We had planned to finalize the work for the show and send it off to Paris for the publication of the brochure, but right after dinner, as we were about to resume our work, Kylie received a call. I glanced at her screen but couldn't identify the caller. She quickly stood and retreated to the bathroom. When she emerged, she looked stunning, but her demeanor had shifted; a jittery energy surrounded her. Half an hour later, she checked her phone again, stood, and announced she had to leave.

"I thought you were staying," I remarked, unable to mask the accusatory tone in my voice.

"I know, but I need to go see someone."

"Who are you seeing?"

"No one you know."

"Jeff?"

"No. I told you, you don't know him." Kylie got irritated. "Don't panic, okay? There's nothing going on."

"Who's Paul?" The words flew out of my mouth.

Kylie's expression hardened for a brief second. She gave me a long, unreadable stare before releasing an exasperated sigh. "You've been speaking with my mother, haven't you?"

My silent gaze confirmed her suspicion.

"What did she tell you?"

"Who is he."

Kylie took a moment, as if searching for a suitable preface to her story, before ultimately surrendering to bluntness. "You want to know who Paul is? I'll tell you. He's the father of the two girls I was tutoring. I stopped because he fell for me."

"And were you in love with him?"

"Was I in love with him? I guess I was. For a while. But then he became obsessed with me and wanted to leave his wife... so, I had to put an end to it."

A bitter taste surfaced in my mouth. I was fuming with anger, and her nonchalant demeanor added fuel to the fire.

"And how does your mother know about this?"

"Because... he was hurt and he lost it. He would come and look for me at home." Kylie's voice escalated with frustration. "Look, he's a great guy, okay. I really cared for him, but we knew it wasn't going anywhere, so I stopped. It's over, okay? It was over before I met you."

"So, how many were there?" I asked, attempting to restrain anger.

Kylie shook her head and emitted a disagreeable sound.

"Were you sleeping with him?"

"Yes, I was. For a while." Kylie took a minute to read my anger. "And how many women where you sleeping with before I came into your life?"

In just over two years, Kylie had dismantled the libertine persona I had taken a lifetime to establish. How quickly I had retreated, sheltering myself within a frame of prudish petit bourgeois morality. I was ashamed of myself, and yet I couldn't stop myself from asking, "So, what's the difference between that relationship and this… what we have now? You know and I know it's not going anywhere."

"You really are an asshole, you know that. You know why I left him? Because I lost respect for him. His love for me made him a pathetic man. Maybe it was my fault. Maybe that's what I do. Maybe I bring out the worst in people."

I shook my head and turned away, either to escape her devastating beauty or to hide my own pitiful existence. The newly styled hair, the eyeliner, the lipstick, the barely noticeable blush… They were clear indicators she was meeting someone.

"Why are you doing this, Jules?"

I lit a cigarette and took a moment to contemplate. "You know what, I don't think I can do this anymore."

"Do what? What are you talking about?"

"The inevitability of it all is suffocating. I can't live in this constant fear. I think we should call it quits. I don't think we should see each other anymore."

Kylie stared at me, her eyes smoldering, her expression one of devastation. "So, you're saying you don't want to see me anymore? Is that what you're saying?"

I hung my head in silence. Kylie picked up her bag and began to walk out. "I'll come for my things later." She stopped at the door, perhaps waiting for me to change my mind. Then, reaching for the doorknob without meeting my gaze, she muttered, "Take care of yourself, okay?"

"I'm sorry," I mumbled, hanging my head.

"No, you're not," fumed Kylie. "You've been sabotaging this from day one. You think you're living in fear? How about me? I have to constantly live with the notion that one day you're going to kick me out of your life, and… that's exactly what you're doing right now."

"Are you fucking kidding me?" I raised my voice. "I'm the one who's been scared shitless of losing you."

"Yes, and that's exactly why you want to stop this, because the fear of losing me is killing you," she yelled. "A preemptive strike! Is that what this is?"

"That's not what I'm doing," I said, alarmed by the fragility of my own voice.

"Then what exactly are you doing?"

"I have no fucking idea, okay? All I know is that I can't live in fear anymore."

"Fear of what?"

Good question. What was I really afraid of? Was I afraid of her disappearing from my life, or was I afraid of losing her in the mundane routine of a compliant, conventional family life that would follow having her, or rather the permanency of having her? How could I tell her that the fear of watching her wilt and become a tame, domesticated person in front of my eyes was far more painful than her absence? In fact, I probably needed her to disappear for me to remember her exactly as she was today, sitting in front of me at that very moment.

"Fear of what?" Kylie shot again. "Remember what you told me when we first met? He who fears suffering, suffers already because he fears. You wrote that quote – whoever it belongs to – in my fucking sketchbook with big, bold letters. I have it right here, in my backpack. But obviously you think there's something beautiful and noble in suffering. Maybe you need all that angst for your art, maybe your suffering fuels your creativity, but me, I can't create when I am depressed. Love is supposed to be a beautiful thing, but you're turning it into a miserable experience. Well, I'm not going to stay here and wallow with you in booze and smoke. You want me to leave, I'm leaving you."

"If you leave me, can I come too?"

Kylie shook her head, ignoring my feeble attempt at making her smile.

"Can I leave myself behind and come with you?" I asked, trying to amend my previous statement.

"Why would you do that?"

"Because you're my muse," I said, instantly recognizing the absurdity of my timing.

"No, I'm not," she replied, her arms limply hanging, her words dry, void of all traces of tenderness. "If I were your muse, you would be cherishing what you have instead of constantly sabotaging it."

"How can I not fear, when I know that one day you will find someone your age, marry him, and have kids?"

"One day! One day I might go blind or lose my legs in an accident or get cancer and die. But until then I want to live the moment," yelled Kylie, pushing me aside. "You know what? You're absolutely right. It's unrealistic of me to expect you to forget that this is only an episode in our lives and that one day I will actually want to be married and have kids. It's true, even though I never talk about it. I do think that you're thirty years older than me and you will die one day. So, you're right. Let's just stop this right now before we start hating each other's guts." Kylie took a deep breath. "I have to go."

"Please stay. I can't imagine my life without you."

"Are you kidding me? That's all you've been doing, imagining your life without me and preparing yourself for it. Anyway, I really need to go. I don't want to argue with you now."

"I don't want to argue either. I promise, I won't," I implored.

"I need to go, and if you want to know where I'm going, I'm meeting Jeff. He wants to meet me to brainstorm some ideas regarding their band. And if you want to know why I didn't tell you, it's because you would never understand. I really don't need to lie to you anymore."

Shaking my head, I tried to speak, but knowing my words would make no difference, I instead followed Kylie out. That's when I noticed a young man casually leaning against an impressive-looking motorcycle, engrossed in his phone. Upon seeing us, he swiftly pocketed his device and greeted us with a subtle smile.

"Jeff, meet Julian," Kylie introduced us.

Jeff responded with a firm handshake. "Pleasure meeting you. Kylie's told me quite a bit about you."

Tall and slender, Jeff stood about my height with long, wavy blond hair cascading over his shoulders. He sported an orange T-shirt, its graphics indecipherable, paired with tattered jeans. A prominent tear showcased his right knee, leading me to muse about how chilly his balls might get when cruising on his motorcycle. His face radiated a certain intelligence, an allure, and a week-old stubble lent a masculine edge to his otherwise slightly effeminate features.

"The pleasure is all mine," I returned, clasping his hand in a courteous two-handed grip. "We finally meet. Would you like to come in?"

"Oh, no, thanks. Some other time. We're already late," he replied, his eyes flicking toward Kylie. "Ready?"

"Ready," Kylie confirmed. She gave me a quick peck on my cheek – a token kiss, a sad one, designed to assure any observer that there was no depth to our bond. She then slipped on her helmet and swung onto the motorcycle, wrapping her arms around Jeff. As they sped off, the motorcycle's roar echoed in my ears, then died down, leaving me with an odd sensation of painful relief. I couldn't help but believe that Kylie had finally provided me with a valid excuse to break free from my addiction to her. Yet the image of Kylie, tightly clutching Jeff on the motorcycle, was imprinted on my mind and impossible to erase. The transformation of Jeff from an abstract figure to a real person filled me with terror, as once more I faced the specter of myself as a murderer. Did I wish for Jeff to die? To my own horror, I had to admit, I most likely did. With all my heart, I wished for Jeff – the only person on earth who could possibly save me – to vanish from the face of the earth.

It's fascinating how the moment I tried to will myself not to think about Jeff, that's all I began to do. Paul was a lost case, I knew it was over, but Jeff lingered in my mind and wouldn't let go of my thoughts. I knew thinking about him would be condemning him to death, so I refused to see or talk to anyone for five days. All I did was drink, smoke pot, and unsuccessfully force myself to sleep. Without Kylie, the idea of exhibiting my works in Paris had lost its appeal. I despised the phone, yet I carried it with me everywhere in the house with the hope that Kylie might call. I was tempted to call her every minute, yet I resisted the temptation, not because my dignity would not allow me, but because I was horrified by the thought of pissing her off even more. Where there is love, there is no dignity. I was ready to humiliate myself to no end, but not at the cost of losing her respect.

To do something drastic and break the spell, I called Paola. I had ignored the two messages she had left but was hoping she was still in town. Ironically, I was relieved when there was no answer. Having no desire to work on large canvases, I spent most of my time doodling, and within a matter of weeks I filled two large notepads with all kinds of sketches.

Kylie's group show took place in a small gallery on La Cienega. I hadn't laid eyes on her for weeks, and being around people wasn't what I was yearning for. Still, I was certain that she anticipated my presence, and I was equally certain that my absence would irreparably destroy what was left of our already damaged relationship.

The venue was swarming with a youthful, trendy crowd, most of whom were there for the free wine and casual mingling. Amid the sea of people, only three paintings caught my eye: Kylie's brilliant pieces. She didn't hide her elation upon seeing me. Navigating her way through the dense crowd, she gave me a long squeeze, kissed my cheeks, and gestured toward the paintings, waiting for my reaction. I was familiar with one of the pieces, but the other two were new to me. They were bold, raw, dynamic pieces – perhaps a little too busy for my taste, yet undeniably youthful and audacious.

"You like them?"

"I love them."

"Really?"

"Yes. I have no reason to lie. I love all three of them. You're going somewhere very exciting. I'm truly proud of you."

Her smile broadened, and she planted a soft kiss on my cheek. After extending my warmest congratulations and sharing a brief moment with Luna, who also seemed thrilled to see me, I moved aside to observe Kylie passionately discussing her pieces with an older couple who seemed genuinely fascinated.

"Oh, I love this work." Kylie gestured to the painting that had caught the couple's interest. "This piece is particularly significant to me because I painted it during a transformative period in my life."

"How so?" inquired the woman.

"This is when I had just fallen in love and we had our first fight," she said without missing a beat. "To me, red is the color of femininity, and white represents masculinity, which is quite dominant in our society in a very inherent way."

Luna shot me a conspiratorial look, her eyes sparkling with mischief. "What a bullshitter! She's good, isn't she?"

I shook my head and smiled.

"She has already sold the other two pieces, and I guess this one's on its way."

"Good for her."

Kylie shook hands with the couple and turned to me. "Okay, I know I'm not supposed to explain my work, but... look at them. Now they think there's a story behind the painting, and... I bet they feel a deeper connection to the piece they're about to hang in their home."

Suddenly, two hands with plump, short fingers playfully covered my eyes from behind, and a familiar female voice chimed, "Guess who?"

When I finally managed to turn around, I saw my old friend Hermine beaming at me from almost a foot lower than my eye level. Hermine was my first love in Los Angeles, the daughter of a well-known Armenian businessman, born in Iran and raised in Germany. She had studied art history at UCLA and had carved out a reputation as an accomplished interior decorator.

"What are you doing here?" Hermine hollered over the gallery hubbub, keeping my hand in hers.

"I'm here to see my… friend Kylie's work," I yelled, pointing at Kylie, who had been observing us intently.

"Kylie, Luna, this is Hermine, one of my oldest friends."

"Yes, I remember Jules talking about you," said Kylie, extending her hand for a shake. "Pleased to meet you."

"So, what are you doing here?" I asked.

"Oh, I was supposed to be here with my friend Linda, but she had a last-minute emergency call and couldn't make it," she explained, locking arms with me. "So, what are you doing after this?"

"After this? Going home, I guess."

"Do you want to have a drink somewhere?"

"I better go home," I said, failing to invent a more convincing excuse.

"Oh, come on, one drink. Why don't I come over?"

I could see Kylie turn to Luna with a silent scoff.

"So, how's Alex?" I diverted the conversation as Hermine began to pull me away.

"Oh, we got divorced three years ago," she responded with surprising cheer, still clutching my arm.

Was I reciprocating Hermine's advances? Was I unwittingly flirting back? Probably. That's who I am, but I'm sure I had no intention of starting anything with her. However, when I saw Kylie grab Luna's arm and disappear in the crowd, I was hit with a wave of resentment and allowed myself to be dragged away by Hermine.

I did not sleep with Hermine. I didn't, even though part of me wanted to, if only to break Kylie's spell and cause serious, irreparable damage to our relationship. I could sense that Hermine was eager to reignite the old flame, but despite the intoxicating haze surrounding us, neither Hermine nor

I acted on it. Instead, we had snacks, smoked pot, and drank a lot. By midnight we were so stoned that I couldn't let her drive home. In a drunken stupor, she ranted mostly about her ex-husband, cried – apparently that's what she does when she's happy – and then drifted into a deep slumber. To be honest, we did do some not-so-heavy petting, but for some reason, neither of us could, or would, take it further. The next day, when she was leaving, we promised to catch up again, knowing well that we never would.

Days later, having not heard from Kylie, I texted her, praising her exhibition and expressing how proud I was of her. The following day I received a seething text from her: "Thank you. I hope you had fun with your friend Hermit, Herman, or whatever her name is."

Her message left me shattered. I decided to eschew any further texting or calling and attempted to distract myself by reverting to a habit from my past: spending my days watching old Westerns on TV.

My friend Lucy visited me a few days later and was shocked at the state she found me in.

"Get up. Get up and get dressed," she insisted, urging me to shower first. She brewed some coffee, watched me shave, then took me to Jack's.

"Okay, I know what you're thinking. You're assuming I'm about to start lecturing again. Well, I'm not. I'm just going to sit here, stay quiet, and watch you wallow," Lucy said, observing me carefully. And since I had nothing to say, we sat in silence for a while, me forcing down the food, she desperately trying to think of something not to say.

"Look, I think you're smart enough to know what you're doing. I know I'm not supposed to talk, but honestly, you were the last person I thought would self-destruct like this," she said, finally breaking the heavy silence.

"Self-destruct?" I echoed, a bitter smile on my face. "What does that even mean? What don't you understand? Is it the age difference? Is it a crime to love someone younger? She's not a teenager, for Christ's sake. She's more mature than many older people I know. Why is it a sin to love someone beautiful, charming, and intelligent? Because it feels too good? She approached me, for fuck's sake. I warned her about the complications. What do you want me to do – feel elated that I'm kicking her out of my life? She makes me happy! What's wrong with that?"

"Happy? Ha!" Lucy scoffed. "You don't even know what happiness means. You're like a gypsy who's happy when it rains because he knows there will be sunshine afterward, but he's sad when it's sunny, because he knows it will rain eventually."

"Why a gypsy?"

"I don't know. My father used to say that. Apparently, that's how gypsies are."

"Why?"

"The fuck should I know! It's entirely irrelevant," Lucy retorted, almost shouting. She took a deep breath, started to say something, but then shook her head and dismissed the thought.

After lunch, we went for a long walk before she dropped me home.

As I was heading in, my heart stuttered when I spotted Kylie's car parked across the street. Indeed, I found her sitting on the steps near the door, her eyes red and puffy from crying. I sat next to her, and the moment I put my arm around her and kissed her cheek, she broke down. "Jeff is dead," she barely managed to whisper.

"What?" I asked, in shock, even though I had clearly heard her.

"Jeff... died. Two days ago. His sister called me this morning," Kylie stuttered through her sobs.

"How? What happened?"

"I don't know. She said it might have been road rage. No one knows exactly what happened. He was shot on his bike late at night on his way home from rehearsal."

Even though a part of me had been bracing for such news, I had genuinely hoped it wouldn't come to pass. Not just because Jeff had left a favorable impression on me, but also because I had started to identify with him, viewing him more as a comrade in the struggle of love rather than a competitor.

"Come on, let's go inside," I suggested, helping her to her feet and walking her into the studio.

Kylie collapsed onto the sofa and continued crying. I poured us both a glass of whiskey and tried to soothe her. In her eyes, I thought I detected more shock than grief, which should have alleviated some of my guilt. Yet the notion of having inadvertently caused the death of an innocent person was too painful to contemplate.

Kylie scanned the room, walked past the discarded brushes with their dried paint, shot me a reproachful look, and settled back into her usual spot on the left side of the sofa. "He was such a good soul. Who could do such a thing? I know, he could be a jerk at times, but he was harmless. And he loved me so much," she lamented between sobs.

I felt horrendous and detestable. If I had lacked a compelling reason to stay away from her before, what had just happened provided more than enough reason to completely extricate myself from her life. My only relief lay in Kylie's blissful ignorance of my previous murders.

I don't think we ever spoke of or even mentioned Jeff's name again. Kylie downed her entire glass of whiskey and drifted into sleep. I attempted to work on a piece that had been troubling me for some time, but realizing I was making no progress, I abandoned the attempt and continued to drink. When Kylie awoke, she seemed less troubled. I ordered some pizza, we drank a bit more, and I assured her that our upcoming trip to Paris was just what we needed to get out of the funk we were in.

8

Vahan calls me, grumbling about our mother's health. He informs me that she's not eating properly and has noticeably lost weight, then insists that I talk to her. I'm aware of her stubbornness and know a conversation won't change much, but I agree anyway. She reassures me that she's eating fine and there's no cause for concern.

"But Vahan says you've lost a lot of weight and you look sick."

"I'm fine. Vahan should worry about Shant. The poor child looks skeletal."

A wave of worry sweeps over me. "Is he sick?"

Mother dismisses my question with an annoyed scoff. I ask her to hand the phone to Vahan.

"What's the matter with Shant?" I inquire.

"No one knows. They say it's some kind of food poisoning. He's been suffering from diarrhea and vomiting for the past three days. Today they did all kinds of tests. We're waiting for the results."

An intense wave of fear comes over me, and I can't help but go over the past few days of our Paris trip. I urge him to call me as soon as they find out what's going on.

Conversations wear me out. I spend over two hours chatting with a collector visiting with Roland to review some of my available pieces. About an hour after they leave, Roland rings up and informs me that the collector was highly impressed with my work and intends to return with his wife to choose at least one piece. "I'm thrilled I came," he remarks. "Why were you hiding these new pieces from me? They're magnificent. I adore them. You've finally found some color again. This is exactly what people want. Color. Keep doing what you're doing."

Just as I'm about to sit down and write, Lucy saunters in, carrying two plastic bags brimming with food. "When was the last time you had *chikufteh?*" she questions, unloading the bags.

"It's three in the afternoon," I say. "Too late for lunch and too early for dinner. You know my eating routine."

"I call this a 'dunch,' a blend of the two. It's my mother's acclaimed chikufteh, specially prepared for you." She then steps in front of the painting I've just completed and covers her mouth in awe. "Wow. This is stunning. It's so fucking good. If you're looking for a place to hang it, I have the perfect wall."

"Merci."

"So, you're painting, and writing now…"

I respond with a nod.

"You look rejuvenated," she observes, biting into her bread. "This is the best I've seen you in a long time. What changed?"

"I've been taking long strolls and eating right and haven't had a drink for days," I say, bringing the coffee to the table.

"Wonderful. You're finally getting your shit together. I told you, this whole experience is going to make you a stronger person. You're going to be just fine."

I nod, and I think to myself, Herr Nietzsche, you were absolutely right when you declared, "That which does not kill us makes us stronger." But then again, I'd prefer to be weak and happy than strong and miserable. Come on, admit it: strength implies trouble. It's a consolation for suffering. And you, Socrates, *agapimu*, did you really say a good wife makes a happy man, while a bad wife makes a philosopher? Well, I got news for you, my friend, a good *life* makes a happy person, a bad one turns you into a philosopher. Philosophy and strength – same shit, crutches to help you walk through life's treacherous terrains.

Kylie was in seventh heaven when we got to Paris. Her vivacious spirit had made a comeback. She found everything fascinating, wonderful, and romantic: the streets, the cafés, the museums, the galleries, my friends, and just about every person we met, including my mother, who was not an easy person to warm up to.

"*Comme tu es belle,*" said my mother, kissing her on her cheeks, but a minute later, in the kitchen, as she was making coffee, she said, "What are you doing with this girl? When are you going to grow up? She's not even Armenian."

"Mom, please don't start."

My mother studied my face for a long moment. "There's something very familiar about her. She looks like someone I know."

I suddenly remembered that I had forgotten to tell Kylie not to mention anything about being Lisa's daughter, but I tried to comfort myself with the thought that she had enough sense not to bring it up.

"I can't believe you haven't visited me for ten years."

"That's not true. I was here only four years ago."

"Yes, and I saw you five times during your entire stay."

"I stayed two weeks and you saw me every single day."

My mother shook her head, determined that my statement did not deserve an answer. For years I had convinced myself that I have developed enough nerve not to let her get to me, but she would prove me wrong every single time.

My brother, Vahan, who had walked into the kitchen, winked at me, signaling me to ignore her, poured a glass of water for Kylie, and walked out.

Vahan had warned me before my trip that mother, now losing her hearing and sight, had become even more intolerable since both her poodles had died.

"So, how are you, Mrs. Varjabedian?" Kylie asked when we took our seats with our coffees in my mother's small, crowded living room.

Kylie looked vibrant and incredibly beautiful. I was impressed by the way she pronounced our last name.

"*Malheureusement, je ne parle pas l'anglais,*" said my mother, almost boasting.

"She says, 'Unfortunately I don't speak English,'" translated my brother.

"Oh, that's fine. I just wish I could speak French," said Kylie. "Your son here has been trying to teach me, but I don't think he has the patience for it."

"He should teach you Armenian," said my brother, without looking at me.

"That too," agreed Kylie.

My mother looked like a black-and-white Modigliani painting: ashen, pallid, hardly able to support her head with her long neck. She had obviously made an attempt to look her best, wearing her long floral dress – a dress she had probably not worn in over half a century – her pearl necklace, its matching earrings, and her high-heeled shoes.

"Jules has spoken so much about you," Kylie said, raising her voice in hopes of being understood better.

Vahan translated.

My mother gave me a chastising look. She always hated it when people called me Julian or Jules. To her I would always be Hovsep. "I wonder what you've told her," she said in Armenian, a derisive smile on her face.

Kylie looked at me askance, expecting me to translate. I did.

"All good things. He loves you so much," Kylie said, feeling a little uncomfortable.

The apartment looked like it had been kept intact. No detectible evidence of Vahan living under the same roof, at least not in the living room or the kitchen. I rose to peek into our old bedroom, then headed to the bathroom to wash my face. The smell of the cheap lavender soap sent a wave of arousal through me. It was the same soap we had used when my mother used to bathe me, the same soap I washed my face with every night, the same soap I used to masturbate with. Suddenly, a loud thud from upstairs shook the entire apartment. I quickly dried my face with a towel and rushed out. "What was that?"

My mother shook her head ruefully. "That's the new neighbor upstairs. The man has lost it. He has gone completely crazy."

Upstairs was where my aunt, Anahit, used to live with my grandmother Zarouhi. Anahit and my mother had never gotten along, but I had always found solace in her presence. I used to spend hours in her room listening to her read me the classics, such as *The Count of Monte Cristo*, *Les Misérables*, and *The Hunchback of Notre Dame*, all in Armenian. It was only a few years later, when I was preparing to translate them into French for my friends, that I realized they were all originally written in French.

I had just returned the towel to the bathroom and stepped out when the front door swung open. My nephew,

Shant, filled the doorway. At twenty-six, he was tall and handsome, and his disarmingly warm smile immediately sparked a twinkle in Kylie's eyes. He halted in the doorway, arms wide open and beaming. Swiftly, he brushed back his hair with his fingers, met me halfway across the room, and pulled me into a bear hug, peppering kisses on my cheeks. "Man, you haven't aged one bit," he remarked, looking me up and down. He then turned to Kylie, gave her a kiss, and took the armchair opposite me.

"Look at you," I said. "You look fucking amazing."

"He looks so much like you that I keep calling him Hovsep," said Mother.

"And who are you?" asked Shant, nodding at Kylie.

"Me?" Kylie asked, looking at me with a smile.

"Kylie is my... friend," I hesitated, unsure of the right descriptor.

"*Mais elle est si belle,*" said Shant, looking at her flirtatiously.

"He thinks you're beautiful," I translated.

"He's not too bad looking either," Kylie responded, laughing.

Shant thanked her and strolled to the kitchen. "Where's my coffee?"

"Okay, so Shant is Vahan's son, which makes him my nephew," I explained. "Vahan is divorced and lives here with mom."

"Shant stays with his own mother, but he's here almost every day," Vahan interjected.

"So, do you like your hotel?" Shant emerged from the kitchen to ask. "It's nice, no?"

"We love it," I said, trying to skirt the sensitive issue of not staying with my mother.

"Great, I'm free for nearly ten days," said Shant. "I can show you around, take you wherever you want."

"Perfect, we can finally spend some quality time together," I replied.

"I'm normally home after six." Vahan yawned, the wear of the past four years etched in his thinning hair and deepening wrinkles. His divorce and living with mother had weighed heavy on his shoulders, giving him a visible hunch. "Is this your first time in Paris?" he asked.

"Yes, and I'm already in love," Kylie answered.

"We love Paris too, but it's becoming the city of the rich. Life here is not easy," Vahan added. "Overcrowded, expensive…"

"Paris will always be Paris," Shant interjected. "I'll show you a Paris you'll never forget."

Since I was busy with the gallery almost every day, working on last-minute arrangements, invitations, and interviews, supervising the stretching and the framing of the works, I did not insist that Kylie spend her days with me. Shant was the perfect tour guide. In a couple of weeks, she had managed to see all the major galleries and museums during the days. At nights, tired from my work, I would retreat to our hotel room as Kylie continued exploring Paris nightlife with Shant and his friends.

For the first time in my life, I felt my age. As much as I tried to catch up with them, I couldn't. I had no problem with drinking and smoking, but the loud music and not sleeping until the wee hours of the day was too much to handle.

It would have been unfair to expect Kylie to spend time with my mother, so I had to spend a few nights a week alone with her, especially when I realized how my presence rejuvenated her. Despite this, I was still a disappointment to my mother. The facts that I don't have a single painting hanging at the Modern Art Museum of Yerevan, that she sees nothing distinctly Armenian about my appearance, and that I am once again with an *odar* woman still hurt the very core of her existence. But at least she seemed to have resigned herself to reality and tried to avoid bringing up sore topics as much as she could.

Since I was watching everything with Kylie's virgin lenses, even when she wasn't around, I felt like a tourist in my own hometown and found Paris far more charming than I had ever perceived. For the first time in my life I was proud of my Paris, and I couldn't wait to show off the city that had let me go without displaying an iota of remorse.

Kylie was happy. She loved spending time with Shant, and she was in such a dreamy, amorous mood, that every night, no matter how late she or we got back to the hotel, she couldn't wait to make love to me. By the end of the second week, I was worn out from playing the part of the youthful, romantic tourist. Of course, nothing about the exhibition went as planned, which did not prevent the slow deterioration of my frame of mind.

The gallery was too small for my works, and the show looked too crowded. Guillem, the gallerist, had to leave three of my favorite pieces out. As promised, he had organized a pre-opening night for his serious collectors, but some eighty people showed up to buy a total of four works. Vahan's warning about the gallery's condition had been correct. My infatuation with Kylie and the idea of impressing her with a Paris exhibition had blinded me to this reality.

Until then, I had been oblivious to the feeling of anxiety. In fact, the concept of anxiety had always seemed ludicrous to me. Nothing – and I mean nothing – was weighty enough to resist the numbing effects of a couple glasses of whiskey and a joint. But now, I didn't need a doctor to diagnose me with anxiety. I would awaken each morning around three o'clock to a racing heart and spells of dizziness. My thoughts would spin uncontrollably, obsessive ideas taking hold and crowding out all else. The terror of inadvertently causing harm to my nephew haunted me. I adored the kid and couldn't fathom causing him any pain, yet I knew I had no control over my thoughts. I yearned for the whole thing to be over and longed to leave Paris before any harm could befall him or the people around me. I knew I should return home, isolate myself in my studio, and maintain my relationships from a safe distance – nothing more than lukewarm and civil.

On Sunday, I took Kylie to Le Marais for breakfast at Café Hugo, in Place des Vosges. After our meal, we strolled back along Rue de Rivoli and stopped where my father's shoe store used to be. Now a clothing shop selling inexpensive men's sport jackets, it was closed, but I spotted a Middle Eastern–looking man inside sorting jackets with a hooked rod.

"This used to be my father's store," I told Kylie, shielding my eyes as I peered through the window. The man, presumably the owner, waved his hand and yelled, "*C'est fermé. Nous sommes fermés.*"

I returned his gesture with a thumbs-up.

My father was the son of genocide survivors who arrived in Marseille in 1922, and about a decade later, they relocated to Paris, where my great-uncle had settled. He had worked for Uncle Souren's humble shoe factory before opening his own shoe store here on Rue de Rivoli. Two of his friends, Mourad and Serop, had set up their stores next to his – Mourad selling watches, Serop peddling ladies' handbags. This corner had morphed into a mini-Armenia, always abuzz with friends and relatives. Across the street, Monsieur Martin, the Basque owner of Martin's Bistro, had learned how to make Armenian coffee for his Armenian customers.

Serop's handbag store had shut down years ago, but Mourad's watch shop, closed on Sundays, still stood, and four years prior, Mourad was thrilled to see me when I visited.

Kylie proposed we have a snack and coffee at Martin's Bistro. A Chinese man, presumably the new owner, was sweeping the floor. Nothing about the place reminded me of the bistro I remembered. It looked dirty and untidy, and the food on display in the counter was far from appetizing.

"*Bonjour, Messieurs Dames*," the owner muttered, pushing back his thick glasses.

I greeted him back with a "bonjour" and turned to Kylie. "Do you know where the word 'bistro' comes from?"

"No, but I have a feeling you're about to tell me."

"Some believe that during the Russian occupation of Paris in 1814, after the Napoleonic Wars, Russian soldiers, while ordering coffee at these small cafés, would sometimes yell 'Bistro, bistro,' meaning 'Hurry up.'"

"Really? Huh… how fascinating…" Kylie imitated a cartoon character, then perused the menu behind the counter and sneered. "You know what, let's just have coffee and some water."

We placed our order and sat outside, under the warm sun.

"What's wrong, baby?" Kylie asked, holding my hand.

"Nothing," I paused, my gaze wandering the streets where my youth was buried. "So much has changed. I've spent my entire childhood here, on this street, around that church. You see that shop over there? I was arrested with my friend Vazken for shoplifting. We must have been fifteen years old. Vazken was a character. He believed that he was born with two dicks, but his parents had asked the doctor to cut off one of them. So, he had a serious grudge against his parents. He visited me in L.A. ten or twelve years ago. He had become a successful businessman. Then there was Valerie, the first girl I was in love with. She used to get so upset at me for hanging around with her father, Monsieur Dubois, who had been a close friend of André Breton. I always wonder what happened to her." I gave myself a dramatic pause and lit a cigarette. "This is where… I found my father dead."

"What do you mean? In the shoe store?"

I nodded. "Yes. I found him in the little room in the back. I was eleven years old. He had died of a heart attack."

Kylie squeezed my hand, a quiet sympathy dancing in her eyes. "That's tough, especially for a kid. I'm so sorry."

"My parent's relationship was pretty shitty. My father was lively, energetic, and charming – the very opposite of my mother, and we all knew that he was in love with another woman. So, he was miserable."

"Well, may be your mother was miserable because of that."

"Probably. Or it could be that the bitterness came from the onset of their marriage, because my father had never gotten over his love of the other woman. Or it could simply be that my mother was a sour person, and that's why my father looked for love somewhere else. All I know is after my father's death, we hardly ever talked about him."

"Did you ever meet the other woman?"

"Yes. I did. She used to come and watch us at school. I remember, she used to sit at the café down the street from where we lived, smoke cigarettes, drink coffee, and wave at us every time Vahan and I passed by on our way home from school."

"I wonder what happened to her."

"I don't know. I think about her all the time. Who was she? What did she do? Is she still alive?"

The Chinese owner brought the coffees and the waters, attempted a smile, then disappeared into the shop.

"Vahan and I hated the woman. We knew something was going on. My mother and father were at it almost every night, yelling and screaming. My father would disappear for a few days, then come home, and everything would be on repeat. Can you imagine what my poor mother must have gone through?"

"How about the other woman? She must have suffered so much."

I nodded.

"Well, this was one of the worst coffees I ever had," said Kylie, grimacing.

"You know what's supposed to be the best coffee in the world?"

"What?"

"Kopi Luwak, from Indonesia. A friend of mine brought it to me a while ago. Apparently, the island of Sumatra is famous for this coffee. These little animals called *luwak*, which are a cross between a fox and a monkey, live in the trees, and their favorite food is the red, ripe coffee cherry. They eat the cherries, which then undergo a chemical treatment and fermentation process during digestion… and of course, they come out with the animal's shit. The farmers collect the beans from the forest, wash them, roast them, grind them, and sell them."

Kylie looked at me skeptically.

"I'm serious," I continued. "Luwak coffee is considered the most flavorful and richest-tasting coffee in the world. It is also the most expensive coffee on the market. Apparently the luwaks know how choose and eat only the very best cherries, and that is why the coffee has such a rich flavor."

"Amazing."

"Isn't it? I think a good artist is a kind of luwak. Whatever an artist consumes finds its way through the digestive system and comes out in his shit, and people pay top dollars for it."

Kylie laughed. "And the difference between a good artist and a bad one is that a good artist knows how to be selective with his consumption – what they read, watch, or listen to."

"Absolutely. And these days, when we're constantly bombarded by a barrage of words and images, the lines between the trivial and the profound, between the mediocre and the good, have blurred so much that it's extremely difficult to uphold high standards in one's consumption of art and culture."

The Chinese man returned with the bill, squinting at Kylie and me. "Daughter?" he asked, gesturing between us.

I laughed, handing him the payment. "No, mother. She's a vampire. She never gets old."

The man chuckled graciously and walked away.

Kylie looked irresistible at the opening night. She was happy, animated, and in total control as she mingled, talking to potential buyers and making sure I was taken care of. By the time we left, nine pieces had sold. Guillem, however, kept assuring me there was interest in other works, and he was confident he would be able to sell at least four more pieces during the next two weeks.

Of the three reviews that covered the exhibition, two of them were almost copies of the press release that the gallery had sent. One of them said, "Julian Varjabedian is a classical abstract expressionist" – whatever that means – and the other claimed to see a heavy influence of Cy Twombly in my works. The third review was rather well written and highlighted the simplicity and the subtlety of my works: "Varjabedian is a serious painter who has the wisdom not to take himself seriously. There is a silence in his works, punctuated by giggles. The whimsical quality of his works is testimony of his profound understanding of the layers of abstraction."

Kylie thought the review was fantastic and that Joel Castanier had grasped the essence of my paintings. Of course, I never told her that Castanier was one of Guillem's close friends and had been drinking with us two nights prior to the opening of the exhibition.

I met Joel a few days later when I was having drinks with Guillem and asked him what he thought the other critic meant with the term "classic abstract expressionist." He said it's a "bullshit term in circulation these days."

"So, what does it mean?" I asked.

"Basically, any abstract expressionist who's not in the postmodern wave or hasn't found a gimmick with some lame story attached to it, preferably with a political angle. Have you seen all the shit in the galleries these days?"

"You mean here in Paris?"

"I mean everywhere. Here, in New York, in L.A., in Japan... All the conceptual art, pop art... It's ridiculous. You know why? Because there was a time when people who bought art came from old money. They were older, with a little more refined, sophisticated taste. Now people who are buying art are the nouveau riche... mostly kids who have made shitloads of money in IT and don't know what to do with it. They will throw three hundred thousand dollars on a piece-of-shit painting of a cartoon character just because they grew up with it." Joel took a swig from his beer and lit another cigarette. "The art scene in Paris is not what it used to be, my friend. We the French have starved so many artists to death that we have developed a deep-rooted sense of guilt. It's in our unconscious. That's why we're so forgiving toward even very mediocre artists, lest we starve another one to death."

Three days before leaving Paris, Kylie and I, after making love, were chatting in bed when she suggested that we extend our stay. "Can we stay two more weeks?" she said, as she tried to pop a blackhead on my cheek.

I shook my head. I was tipsy and tired, could hardly keep my eyes open.

"Please," sang Kylie.

"No."

"Why not?"

"Because we can't. I need to be back in L.A."

"Why? What's in L.A.? We have nothing urgent to do. Two more weeks."

I shook my head again.

"How about one week?"

"No."

"Will you be really upset at me if I decide to stay?"

"What does 'really upset' mean? If I tell you I will be mildly upset if you stay, then will you stay?"

"Maybe," said Kylie, pouting.

I drew in a deep, uneasy breath.

"Fine," Kylie sulked. "But you have to promise that we'll return soon."

I gave a noncommittal nod.

"Maybe we can live here for a while?"

Not getting a response from me, Kylie nudged my arm. "What? Why can't we?"

"Because living here is not easy. Visiting Paris as a tourist is fun and exciting, but living here is another story."

"Can we live here permanently as tourists?" Kylie asked, taking on her adolescent, impish character.

I shrugged. Can one live life as a tourist? As a person who visits life with an open visa, has nothing better to do, is guided solely by curiosity, and has the luxury to leave any time they want.

"Promise?" Kylie nudged again.

"Yes." I refrained from mentioning that her hair held a faint trace of Shant's scent or that the delicate silver bracelet she wore reminded me of him. There was an extra twinkle in her eyes, possibly ignited by him. I did my best not only to avoid bringing up my nephew but also to banish him from my thoughts. A burgeoning sadness had seeded itself in the most shadowed recesses of my heart, and I could feel its roots boring deeply into my soul.

Two days before the opening of my exhibition, an incident occurred that left me utterly shattered. My plan was to assist Guillem with some last-minute changes at the gallery, but around 7 p.m., he insisted that I should enjoy the evening with friends. Anticipating Kylie's return from her outing with Shant, I intended to take a brief nap, freshen up, and then have dinner with her. However, upon unlocking the hotel room door, I found Shant lounged on the bed, fully dressed, while Kylie was in the bathroom. When she came out and saw me, she was visibly startled. She stopped, regained her composure, and gave me a long embrace. "You're here. I thought you were going to be late. I had such a bad stomachache that we had to come to the hotel. It must be something I ate."

Shant's demeanor remained unchanged. He stood up, kissed my cheeks, then made his way to the kitchen. "I brought some beer. Would you like some?"

"Sure."

I tried my best to suppress any suspicions and acted cheerful and lively. We drank beer and conversed about their day, and after Shant's departure, Kylie and I decided to spend the rest of the evening in. We made love, and despite Kylie's extra tenderness, I felt detached. I was feeling inadequate and drowsy. The notion of causing harm to Shant or even Kylie had implanted itself in my mind, and I feared it would be impossible to discard.

After returning from Paris, I sank into a deep funk, with my insecurities gnawing away at my sense of self. Kylie had grown more irritable, impatient, and assertive, which paradoxically only intensified my love for her, making her more anxious about our relationship.

My desperation to win Kylie's approval had reached a pitiful peak. I was horrified by the immense influence this now twenty-six-year-old woman had over me. I loved Kylie but despised that I was in love with her.

My painting continued, but I found nothing satisfactory in what I created. I would complete a piece, set it aside, start a new one, and a week later, I would find myself painting over the previous work.

"I think I know why you're so frustrated," Kylie proposed one day, observing my visible discontent. "You don't like them because they're ugly."

"Ugly?" I asked, stunned.

"I know, I know, we're not supposed to use the word 'ugly' in art, and I understand everything's subjective and 'ugly' is a relative term, but I genuinely think some things are just ugly as shit. I know Chagall once said the spit that the artist spits is art, but that's bullshit."

"That wasn't Chagall, that was Kurt Schwitters," I corrected. "He said everything an artist spits out is art, and years later Piero Manzoni sold his shit – his actual shit packed in small cans for the price of gold."

"When was this?"

"In the sixties. I swear."

"Well, shit is shit no matter who has taken the shit."

"Well, his shit was recently sold for over a hundred thousand euros at Sotheby's."

"I don't care. It's still shit."

"Manzoni was very young when he died. I think he was in his early thirties."

"I'm sure he died of constipation." Kylie paused, shaking her head apologetically. "You're an incredible artist, Jules, but you've been trying to eliminate everything that's ornate and decorative for so long that you have finally gotten to a point where there's nothing more to eliminate. I think your search for raw, pure work with no intention to please anyone has taken you somewhere where you are deliberately creating work that is not pleasing to the eye. That's because you're scared shitless of creating something that is even mildly agreeable."

I nodded in silence, not sure if I could come up with a defense, but knowing she was right. She had identified the issue with pinpoint precision.

"Think about it, Jules. Maybe this is why so many incredible artists create some really shitty works. All because they're terrified of creating normal, pleasing, agreeable pieces. So, they do exactly the opposite."

Perhaps I was too proud to admit that she had a point. But she already knew, and the triumphant glint in her eyes made her even more irresistible.

Over the next few weeks, I stopped fighting with my hand and allowed it to paint, but nothing very interesting came out. Painting had become an unpleasant chore. Incapable of painting, reading, or watching television, I would spend countless hours sprawled on the sofa, drinking, smoking, and wallowing in self-pity. Then it happened again. Kylie disappeared for four days – an eternity when one is in love. I called, texted, but did not hear back. When she finally showed up, she looked worn out and disheveled. "What are you doing?" she asked, striking a guilty pose by the door.

It's strange how one's body responds when one experiences intense love and anger toward a person simultaneously. Unable to run to her or away from her, I was paralyzed.

"I miss you," she whispered when she realized I had no intention of speaking.

I downed a tall glass of water and trudged to the table.

Kylie threw her bag on the chair near her paintings and stopped me by pressing her forehead to my chest. "I'm sorry."

"Yes. I'm sorry too," I said, holding her limply. "But I finally got the message."

"What message?"

"That it's over. That whatever time you spend with me is not out of love, but out of sheer kindness of your heart. But you know what hurts me more than anything else? The loss of my dignity. That kills me."

"There you go again… with your dignity. Why are you saying that?"

"Why? When a fucking fifty-four-year-old man calls sixty-two times and is ignored, when he salivates like a dog every time he sees the person he loves, when he follows a twenty-six-year-old girl like a sick puppy, when he know he's not wanted and still tries to convince himself that he is misreading the cues – that, my dear, is loss of dignity."

"Stop," Kylie whispered.

"What? Am I lying?"

"I really don't want to argue with you, okay? This is exactly why I don't want to see you anymore. I never seem to do anything right. There's always something that's eating you up. You're never, ever, content. You're never happy. There was a time when all we did was laugh. Now, every time we're together, a sense of heaviness comes over me. Within the three years we've been together, you lost your shine, your levity, and I think it's all because of me. I somehow make you miserable. All my friends are saying the same thing about me."

"Saying what?"

"That I am not myself anymore. I'm always moody and depressed."

"Could it be that's because you're older and more mature? Could it be because you have become a damn good artist? Could it be because you're not the naive, wide-eyed little girl who walked in here three years ago?"

"But I don't like what I have become."

"I warned you, didn't I?"

"This has nothing to do with art. You love being miserable. I've seen it over and over again. Every time things go well, you create a reason to get depressed, because you honestly believe that without angst there is no art."

"Of course there is, but it's feeble, mediocre art. Like the Talmud says, "For we are like olives, only when crushed we yield what's best in us.""

"That's bullshit," Kylie yelled. "It might be true for olives, but not for me. It's okay for an olive to be crushed, because an olive is a fucking olive. It doesn't feel anything. But you're not an olive. You're a human being, and when crushed, you wither, die, and become useless. Look at you! I thought I was your muse. What happened? You haven't been able to create anything for weeks."

"I'm tired. I'm drained." I lit a cigarette and sat down. "Last night I realized that I was never, ever completely happy or content, because it seems to me that all my life I had been searching for you. Then when I finally found you, the fear of losing you made life unbearable."

"But you haven't lost me, Jules. I will always love you. I will always be in your life. No matter what I do, you will always live in me. Your home inside me will always be there for you."

A cold current went through me. "What happened? How did you fall out of love with me?"

Kylie rubbed away the mascara streaking from her damp eyes. "I haven't fallen out of love. I still love you. But I'm trying to be more truthful, to myself and to you. You did it. You finally convinced me that maybe I should be more pragmatic. Maybe I should not tie my fate with yours and end up completely alone twenty years from now when you're gone."

As Kylie perched atop the table and tenderly caressed my cheek, I could only imagine how pitiful I must have appeared.

"You're right," I admitted. "You're absolutely right. What the fuck was I thinking? I'm the elder one here. I'm supposed to be the wiser one. I'm the one who should say your happiness is far more important to me than anything else. I love you and I want you to be happy. Don't let me convince you to stay."

Kylie pressed her lips to the palm of my hand.

"Go," I implored, retracting my hand.

"You once said our relationship has so many different layers. What happens if one of those layers is gone? What if we're no longer romantically involved?" Kylie probed.

"Love gives wings to friendship. Without passion, the fizz will evaporate, leaving what's left flat and dull," I responded, maintaining my composure.

Kylie's eyes welled up again. "That makes me so sad."

"Kylig, there can be no friendship between men and women. Show me an example, and I'll guarantee you one of them is miserable."

Shaking her head frantically, Kylie pleaded, "Don't say that. Please don't say that."

"It's the truth. Romance is the spirit of a relationship. I'm not necessarily talking about sex. I'm talking about a romance that completes all the different dimensions of love." Trying to make it sound as profoundly dramatic as possible, I picked up the bottle of whiskey and gulped down the rest. "Here, now there is no romance. The bottle is empty. And it's okay, we drank it, we got drunk, and now it's over, it's gone, finished. Do the right thing. Don't let me convince you otherwise. It's going to take some time for me to accept your loss, but I'll survive. I will be there for you no matter what. Just give me some time to recover. I'll try not to call you, and if I do, please be courteous but firm with me. Don't let me try to win you back. It's not beneficial for either of us."

Tears and more tears.

Kylie. "I love you."

Me. "You're crying. You're actually crying, Kylig. It's the first time I've seen you cry. Wow. I am touched."

"I've cried before," Kylie sniffled, defending her emotional integrity.

"No, never."

"Of course I have. Many times."

"I have seen you shed tears a few times, but this is what you call 'serious crying.'"

Drying her tears, Kylie fixed a determined gaze on me and asked, "What do you want from me, Jules?"

I could only shake my head.

My vision had blurred, and my esophagus was on fire. "Nothing. I don't want anything. I want you to live your life and have fun doing it. Just tell me one thing, and I want you to be very honest with me."

Kylie's face paled. She nodded, closing her eyes.

"Tell me, that day, at the hotel… Did something happen between you and Shant?"

The reverse of a smile formed on Kylie's face.

"Please be honest with me."

Kylie pursed her lips, inhaled deeply. "He tried to kiss me."

"Tried to?"

"Well, he did kiss me, and I… didn't know what to do… so I… kinda kissed back."

"Kinda? What does 'kinda kissed back' mean? You mean you kissed him." A surge of heat traveled from my neck to my skull, reaching my eyes. I regretted asking the question almost instantly, since I had my suspicions about what the answer would be. And now, I had to deal not only with the heartache of losing her but also with the terrifying thought of killing my nephew. In that moment, all I wanted was to lose consciousness, to simply cease to exist.

Kylie gave me a disbelieving look, shook her head, then took a deep breath, turned around, and walked away, picking up her bag on her way out.

I don't know how long I stayed frozen in place, but as her footsteps faded, I knew this was the end.

9

I am at Tony's, writing, when I get a call from Shant.

"Are you okay? I've been worried sick about you."

"I'm fine," he says, his tone lighter than I expected. "I was a little sick, that's all."

"But your father said…"

"I know, everybody was worried, but I'm fine," he reassures me. "It was just a touch of stomach flu, that's all."

"Well, I'm glad you're feeling better."

He tells me about his new job, complains about his father, then out of nowhere asks, "How's Kylie?"

"She's fine, I suppose. I haven't seen her for over two months."

"How come?"

I have no answer.

"You know, she really loves you," he says, breaking the silence after a long pause. "It's true, she genuinely loves you."

I don't answer, but the pang I thought I had overcome comes back to bite my heart. "Why are you saying that?" I finally ask.

"Because I don't think you realize how much."

"Well, thanks for letting me know."

"*Bisous.*"

"Bisous." I put down the phone, then pick it up again to call Kylie. It's a reflex. The thought process comes later, when I convince myself that I should stick to my decision of staying away from her for the good of both of us.

You know you're really fucked when you can't even muster a fake smile. My facial muscles seemed to have forgotten how to feign a smile, and it seemed that along with this, they had lost the ability to hold back my tears. The smallest things could trigger me: a sappy song, a corny quote, a sentimental movie.... It was as if anything could breach the dam holding back my tears. I had also lost my raison d'être, and for the first time, it occurred to me that I was capable of endangering Kylie's life. I was afraid that in order to make the separation more tolerable, I was festering an unfamiliar anger inside me, and I could only hope that anger would not take over the love I had for her. I went into hibernation for months. Lucy and a few other friends visited me but did not stay long. They all knew I was prone to migraines, so I used the migraine as an excuse and asked them to just let me be. The idea of painting or creating anything seemed more absurd than ever. I had no reason to paint, no desire to impress anyone, and impressing myself seemed to be a ridiculous notion.

I spent most of my time drunk. I remember one afternoon when my friend Ara practically had to break down the door to get me to open it, insisting on dragging me out. I had no desire to talk, so we sat in silence at Tony's and watched couples stroll by, hand in hand, engaged in lively conversation, giggling, basking in the midafternoon sun as they paraded their love, or at least their pursuit of it.

In the last few months of Lee's life, as his infection deteriorated to the point where he was unable to speak or walk, he spent all his time in front of the television, remote control in hand, aimlessly surfing channels. The painkillers had blurred his grasp on reality, and the vacant stare in his eyes made it obvious that his mind was fading, with his body ready to follow suit. Every time I took him to the hospital for his intravenous antibiotic injections, he would sit next to me in the passenger's seat, mimicking the act of changing channels, perhaps under the illusion that the car's windshield was a large television screen, and nothing he saw was worth watching. Now, sitting at an outdoor café and observing the flow of people, I had become like Lee – numb inside – surfing through invisible channels, painfully aware that there was nothing out there worth watching.

Three weeks later, on a Saturday night, around eleven o'clock, after Jacques and Ara had left and I was lying in bed trying to read, I heard a soft knock on the door. It was Kylie's knock. My heart pounded as I hastily put on my pants and opened the door. Kylie stood there, shoulders sagging, eyes smeared with mascara and bloodshot; she was clad in high heels and the black dress I had bought her a few months after we had met. Her hands were tightly clasped together, her black purse hanging limply from her fingers.

We spoke silence for a minute, then she leaned her forehead against my chest, as she always loved to do, and inhaled deeply. "I miss your smell."

I held her tight. "I miss you so fucking much."

We didn't have much to say. We were both exhausted from being caught in the same cycle, and we both knew that there was nothing we could say or do that would make a difference. Our relationship had reached a deadlock, and it seemed we would be stuck in this purgatory indefinitely, waiting for life to choose a path for us.

"Okay, I'm drunk. I was at a party and… I miss you. I called but you didn't pick up."

"You did?"

"Yes, a few times."

"And you drove in this condition?"

"No, I didn't. Adam drove me here."

"Who's Adam?"

"He's the guy I went to the party with."

"That was nice of him."

"Yeah, he's nice. He owns the Greenberg Gallery on La Cienega, the one we love. He's a fan of my work and has offered me a solo show next April," Kylie explained, her tone carrying a hint of apology.

"Good for you," I said, genuinely happy for her. "Your work is good. It deserves to be seen. It took me nearly forty years to find my own voice, and you... I think you're ready. Your work is solid, powerful."

Kylie studied me, attempting to discern the sincerity of my words. "You have no idea how much that means to me."

"Well, it's true." I assured her. "So, what are you doing here? You're going to piss him off."

Kylie held my hand and walked me to the sofa. "Hug me."

I sat next to her, held her head on my chest and, a few minutes later, heard her fall asleep. I have no idea when I, too, finally dozed off, but she was still asleep when I woke up in the morning and brought breakfast for both of us.

We spent the rest of the day together, trying to re-create one of our earlier, cheerful days, but it was apparent to both of us that the damage was irreversible. It felt as if all I was doing was struggling against my urges, which was an impossible task. Every pore of my body yearned for her touch, my mouth ached for her nipples, my eyes for her moist, dreamy stare in ecstasy, and my sex for the wetness of her inside, and yet we didn't even kiss.

In the early afternoon, Kylie insisted that I start working on a piece that had been hanging on my painting wall for the past three weeks.

I put some music on, poured myself a glass of whiskey, and began to paint. By the time darkness fell, I was tipsy and spent. I paused, shared some cold cuts with Kylie, and then told her I had no desire to paint.

"Remember what you told me once? Creating has nothing to do with mood. You paint because you have to."

"I can't. You know what's the most important piece of art ever created? Magritte's *Ceci n'est pas une pipe* – Magritte's painting of a pipe with the inscription underneath saying 'This not a pipe,' meaning this is only a painting of a pipe."

"I know that painting."

"Well, what he meant was, no matter how realistically you paint something, it's still a representation, a painting. It's only art. You understand what I'm saying? All these years I've created art, but I can't do it anymore. I want to live it. Over the past two years, I've come to realize that everything I create will pale compared to the intensity of life."

"Please don't say that, Jules. You have created some of the most profound pieces I have ever seen. Look at your work. Your life is not over. You have so much to look forward to, so much to give. Come on, get up and wash your face."

"I can't. I don't know what to do with the piece anyway. I'm not satisfied with anything I paint."

"Jules, please. Stop feeling sorry for yourself. Please. You're bigger, stronger than this. What am I? Nothing. Don't let me do this to you. I'm not worth it, Jules." Kylie kissed my hand and stared into my eyes for an eternity; then she let go of my hand and sat up.

I was feeling nauseous, intoxicated, and could hardly keep on my feet. I went to the bathroom, washed my face, dried it, and stared in the mirror, towel in hand. The man gazing back at me from the mirror looked twenty years older, frazzled and lost. His hair was receding, his nose ·

swollen, his mouth dry; the expression on his face reminded me of a picture of my father taken in front of his shoe store on Rue de Rivoli, probably the year he died. This was not the man I could allow the woman I worshipped to be with.

When I came out, Kylie was wearing nothing but one of my painting shirts, which looked like a dress on her. Barefoot, she had been painting over my abandoned piece. Was she doing it on purpose, to torture me? I don't know. All I know is watching her was heartbreaking. I lay on the sofa, my head resting on my arm, watching her paint, her hair in an updo, fastened with a brush, another brush in one hand, my water spray bottle in the other, painting and dancing. In less than half an hour, she had transformed my painting into a masterpiece. The colors, the composition, the use of space, the drips... She had become an improved version of me, with the raw energy and the brash overconfidence of a now twenty-seven-year-old.

I was in awe. Kylie had become a bona fide artist, and I knew that my existence in her life now was not only completely irrelevant, but a hindrance to her progress. She was young, talented, beautiful, and charming, possessing something I had never had: the willingness to sell her soul to the highest bidder. Perhaps I'm lying. Perhaps instead of the word "willingness" I should use the word "eagerness," because to be utterly honest with myself, at her age I think I also was willing to sell my soul, but I might have lacked the eagerness or hadn't simply found a buyer for it.

She threw the brush in the water bucket, took a gulp from the whiskey bottle, then came to the sofa, crawled behind me, unbuttoned my shirt, took off my pants, then spooned me, her breasts against my back, her sex caressing my ass, her hands on my chest. She lay there, motionless, breathing against my nape. In that moment, all I wanted was to capture the instant for eternity. Since I couldn't freeze time, I froze myself, and since I couldn't freeze my tears, I sobbed out loud. I cried because I knew that the only way to end this was to wish my own demise. It had to be done; otherwise I was going to jeopardize some other life. And since jeopardizing Kylie's life could not be an option, I had to wish my own demise.

Bukowski, dude, did you really mean it when you said, "Find what you love and let it kill you. Let it drain you of your all. Let it cling onto your back and weigh you down into eventual nothingness"? Did you truly mean it? Didn't you realize that by the time what you adore starts to consume you, your instinct for self-preservation overrides everything? Your love morphs into something unrecognizable, something that, in honesty, might be called loathing, even while your executioner is pressing her sweet, exquisite, moist vagina on the base of your tail. Dude, you're right: all things will kill us, slow or fast, but it's so much more painful when the person killing you is your lover.

He who lives by love dies by love.

The Greeks have eight words for love. I wonder which one of them is the deadly one. The one that kills.

And then it dawned on me: within a fleeting moment, I had become the executioner. I had wished her dead, and as always, the thought clung stubbornly to my existence. It would burrow into my mind, my heart, wherever darkness finds a haven, leading to the destruction of the one person who had worshipped me. Yes, I wanted her dead, but then again, what was life worth without her? If I had truly been her creator, then my creation had in turn shaped me, molded me into what I was: a killer incapable of outliving his own executioner. And so, I needed to die, and with me I needed to take the entire world, because no one, and

I mean no one, was guilty enough to endure the absurd mockery called life, including – or rather, especially – God, who had failed to segregate love from tears.

10

During the past few days, the name "Paul" has kept popping up in my mind. I have no idea if anything has happened to him, the father of the two little girls Kylie was tutoring. I have no desire to find out. I just hope he's alive and well.

We have just returned from a dismal exhibition at the Bergamot Station. I drop off Ara at his car, park my own across the street from Derek's place, and proceed to walk home. It must be past 6 p.m., but it's still daylight. These are the streets where I used to take Lee for his daily walks when he was still capable of walking. He would walk holding my arm with one hand and his cane with the other, his head held high, stopping at every tenth step, looking around in slow motion, smiling at everyone passing by, hoping to strike up a conversation with anyone who would catch his glance. I pick a lemon from the tree that is curiously peeping out of a fence, cross the street, and am about to walk into my driveway when a tall man in a hoodie appears out of nowhere.

"What's that in your hand?" he mutters, surreptitiously surveying the street.

A shudder courses through my body. This will not end well. I see death written all over it. The man in front of me is probably in his late forties but looks much older. He is clean-shaven, well-kept, but there's something deeply unsettling about his green, bloodshot eyes.

"This?" I ask, showing him the lemon in my hand.

The man doesn't hear me. He looks around nervously, then almost whispers in my ear, "Give me your wallet." As he raises his left arm to adjust his hoodie, I notice the glitter of a switchblade in his right hand.

"Give me your fucking wallet," he repeats impatiently. A foul, fetid smell fills the air and permeates my nostrils. It's the smell of a sewer, and it's emanating from him. I reach into the pocket of my jeans, ready to hand him my wallet, when I notice an alarming shift. His eyes, previously sharp and predatory, roll in their sockets. His left arm, which had been threateningly poised, slumps down, heavy and lifeless. His knees buckle under an unseen weight, forcing him into an unsteady kneel. He latches onto my wrist with a desperate grip and, with a guttural rasp, mutters, "Call 9-1-1" – or that's what I decipher from the near-inaudible mumble.

This, I realize with a cold shudder, is what a heart attack – or perhaps a stroke – looks like. He continues to clutch my wrist in a feeble attempt to anchor himself to life, even as his strength rapidly diminishes. Like a marionette with its strings cut, he crumbles, his body collapsing onto his bent knees, propped up only by the white fence behind him.

Pulling my hand from his loosening grip, I retreat a few steps and dial 9-1-1, my hand trembling, my heart pounding.

For what feels like an eternity, I stand vigil by the body. His once-threatening presence now reduced to a pitiful heap on the pavement. Touching him is out of the question. The wailing sirens finally punctuate the eerie silence, and police officers swarm the scene, their grim faces masked by professional detachment. They confirm what I already know: the man is dead. The fire department arrives, taking over the scene with an air of practiced routine. As they cart away the lifeless body, the police launch into a series of questions, their pens poised over notepads. Having gathered what they need, they let me go, leaving me alone with my lingering shock and the ghost of the day's events.

I return home, my legs still trembling, pour myself a glass of whiskey, and survey the studio with a long, exhausted glance: my paintings, Kylie's paintings, the books, the paints, the brushes.... It feels good to be alive. Is there a way to annul the condemnation I have cast upon the world in my moment of despair? I don't know, but I know that I am not ready to die.

I have finished writing my story, and yet, it's not over. I say I have finished it only because I have decided to stop writing. I have stopped because something inside me has decided that love and death should not be synonymous. I have no idea what will happen next: Who knows? Tomorrow I might get into a car accident while crossing the street, a comet might hit the earth and shatter it to pieces, a virus might wipe out the human race, or some madman might decide to press a button and put an end to this whole madness called humanity. Until then, I will be the master of my own destiny. I will breathe the orange blossom–scented air, bask in the sun's warmth, and paint until my arms go numb.

Louis L'Amour, partner, apparently at one point you said there will come a time when you believe everything is finished, and *that* will be the beginning. Did you really get to a point in your life where you believed everything was finished, or was it through a character you had created for one of your Westerns? How can one believe everything is over and yet see a beginning at the same time? I don't know. Perhaps this is a beginning. Perhaps this is the moment I realize how absurd love can be: here I am, desperately clenching my heart to stop it from beating for someone else, while just down the street a homeless man succumbs to an overdose. The director of the CIA plots the downfall of a regime, a distraught mother in Montreal confronts a nurse in a hospital hallway, and a Taliban fighter readies himself with a suicide vest.

Or, who knows, perhaps it all boils down to love. Could it be that the homeless man is sniffing crack because his love has been rejected; the CIA director is obsessed with toppling a regime because he hasn't fucked his wife for three years; the mother in Montreal is pacing in pain because her six-year-old son is dying of cancer; and the Taliban fighter is preparing the vest because he believes that there are seventy virgins waiting for him with open legs in heaven?

I don't know.

I pick up my notebook and leaf through it. What have I done? I have turned a living, breathing experience into mere words.

Ceci n'est pas de l'amour.

This is only a story of love.

The story of a man addicted to love, flattened, suffocated, strangled by his own love for a young woman whose only crime has been to love, albeit, in her own way.

Non, ceci n'est pas de l'amour.

C'est juste l'histoire d'un amour.

I have finally killed love; I have turned a living experience into a memory by preserving it. Why? Was it the only way to relive it? Perhaps. Is that what cowards do – preserve life under the thin veneer of artistry? Perhaps.

I put the notebook down and survey the room. This is my life. This, my life, is the painting I have created by all the decisions that I have made. What would have happened if I had stayed in Paris? What would have happened if I had decided to become an architect instead of a painter? What would have happened if Lisa and I had not separated? What would have happened if I had committed suicide, as I had intended to do twelve years ago, when I was going through a severe bout of depression? What would have happened if I had decided to stay with Kylie and started a family? If I had a brush to paint my life all over again, would I paint over this life and start anew? A thousand times no. I know this is all I'm good for: preservation. Every creation is a preservation of some sort: images, forms, ideas, pictures, thoughts, and stories. As soon as we preserve them, we kill them, embalm them and turn them into art. And yet what does one preserve when one has not lived? How can one preserve the symphony of heartbeats of a fresh love without smelling the singe of one's own heart? How can one hope to capture the delirium of lost love without first plummeting into the depths of one's own madness?

And so, I bring out a new white canvas, pick up a brush, and begin to transform life into art. I paint and...wait for life to make its presence known, with those three timid knocks that spell the beginning, or the end.

Photo: Gor Kirakosian

VAHE BERBERIAN

Playwright, novelist, monologuist, artist, director, and actor,
Berberian is among the most highly regarded intellectuals
within Armenian communities worldwide. His six monologues
have made him a household name, and his plays have been
translated into various languages and staged internationally.
His novels *Letters From Zaatar, In The Name Of The Father
And The Son*, and *Diary Of A Dead Man* have established him
as one of the most respected and widely read contemporary
Armenian writers in the diaspora.

Born in Beirut, Lebanon, Berberian has lived in Los Angeles
since 1977.

Made in the USA
Las Vegas, NV
25 January 2025

16936972R00095